Cecilia needed a ğ

cobwebs loose once ev(

So, today was the

invitation to her wedding -- nei ıu..

and eighth, to be exact, little money-grubbing whore Brykolos, he was *so* proud -- to some child who would worship at her perfectly manicured feet and beg her to turn him for twenty years before that bored her. Bast'd called to refuse the invitation.

After all, he did *know* how the silly ceremonies went.

She'd cried and screamed and called him a reprobate and sixty or seventy other well-loved terms before the real fun started. They were heading into the breaking of things when the elevator grate opened.

"Fucking shit, Bast! What the hell is going on? I could hear you down the street!" Trick looked concerned, the frown making lines appear on his forehead and between his brows.

Bast screamed another volley of insults into the phone and then covered the mouthpiece with his hand. "My sister."

A half smile quirked his sweet's face, making the lines disappear. "I take it you aren't close."

"Not at all, thank goodness." He fired off another shot, making sure to comment on her body odor and general resemblance to a breed of ill-tempered hairy goat.

This is a work of fiction. Names, characters, places, and incidents either are the product of the author's imagination or are used fictitiously. Any resemblance to actual events, locales, organizations, or persons, living or dead, is entirely coincidental and beyond the intent of either the author or the publisher.

Chosen
TOP SHELF
An imprint of Torquere Press Publishers
PO Box 2545
Round Rock, TX 78680

Cover illustration by Pluto
Published with permission
ISBN: 978-1-60370-184-6, 1-60370-184-2

www.torquerepress.com


First Torquere Press Printing: October 2007
Second Printing: June 2008
Printed in the USA

**If you enjoyed Chosen,**
**you might enjoy these Torquere Press titles:**

Long, Black Cadillac by BA Tortuga

Need by Sean Michael

Soul Mates: Bound by Blood by Jourdan Lane

Timeless Hunger by BA Tortuga

Touching Evil by Rob Knight

# *Chosen*
## *by Sean Michael*

Torquere Press Inc.
romance for the rest of us
www.torquerepress.com

Chosen

# Chapter One

Bast liked playing games.

It was just one of the things Trick loved about his lover. He grinned as he settled in with some popcorn and a Star Trek marathon.

He'd sent Bast on a chase. He'd set the whole thing up yesterday, each clue would lead Bast somewhere else for the next clue and eventually, back home again to find him. Hopefully, by the time Bast found him here on their bed, his lover would be starving and horny.

Those were a good combination.

In the meantime, he had bad TV to mock.

It wasn't long before the elevator started creaking and whirring, distracting him from Kirk and Spock.

He looked down at his barely touched popcorn and hit time on the remote, frowning. Surely Bast wasn't back already? He wasn't even naked yet, let alone had the dildo he had planned to be fucking himself with lubed up and ready to go.

The grate didn't rise; there wasn't a sound, just the yellow light pouring out. He put aside his popcorn and stood up slowly, but he couldn't see anyone from the bed.

He quietly made his way over to the elevator. It was empty except for a single, blood-red rose with a tiny key attached by a creamy ribbon, resting fragrant on the floor

Trick grinned. Not only had Bast figured him out way earlier than he'd expected, but his lover was turning the tables on him. Still grinning, he opened the grating and picked up the rose, undoing the bow to get to the key. The little shining bit of metal was familiar, the one to a silver pair of bonds Bast had kept for god knew how long. He turned, heading over to their toy chest where the cuffs should be, when the elevator headed back up.

It didn't take long to find the handcuffs, the only question was -- should he be wearing them or should Bast?

His decision, he guessed, as the game seemed to be passing back and forth between them.

Excitement made his spine tingle and he stripped himself down to skin and then the bed down to the black silk sheets.

After opening the cuffs, he dipped the key in a pot of oil Bast liked and carefully pushed it into his ass. He settled himself gingerly in the middle of the bed and laid the rose across his chest before locking the cuffs around one wrist. He'd just looped the cuffs through the slats on the headboard and locked them around his other wrist when the elevator settled back down again.

The grate opened and a very slinky, very feral, very leather-clad vampire sauntered across the room, long, dark hair loose. Bast might have been over seven hundred years old, but he didn't look a day older than when Trick had first met him in line outside a club. Short and slender, he had dark eyes that could go feral and gold in a heartbeat and that silky hair framed a face as smooth as any teenager's. "Mmm... Sweets."

Trick all but purred at the sight. Fuck, but Bast was sexy. His cock began to fill, sliding along his thigh and up past his hip. He licked his lips. "Hey, baby-boy." His ancient baby-boy.

"Someone was being very, very naughty this evening -- trying to lead me on a wild Trick chase." One finger slid up his calf.

"Are you going to punish me?" he asked, breathless at the simple touch, at the look in Bast's eyes.

"I should." Bast leaned down, licking his shaft once before straddling his body, leather warm against his skin. "The question is, how?"

He arched slightly, stretching out for Bast, letting his head fall back slightly, rubbing as best he could against his lover.

The vampire leaned in, scraping his throat with sharp fangs, teasing. "Such a temptation, Sweets."

He shuddered. "Fuck, Bast. You make me feel so good."

Bast's exhalation was hot, sweet, tongue sliding on his skin. He moaned softly, pushing up toward Bast's mouth, wanting more.

Bast shuddered. "You're trying to make me forget what I am doing, trying to make me need..."

He shook his head. "I'm just trying to get off."

"Mmm... then you'll just have to wait." Bast sat up, stretched, and started rubbing himself through the leather. "My turn first."

Trick whimpered. "Fuck, baby-boy... you're fucking gorgeous." He swallowed hard, wanting to touch, to be touched, at the same time loving watching every move Bast made.

Bast arched, fingers pulling out the long, stiff cock, pumping it slow and easy. "Mmm... feels fucking good, Sweet. You're so fucking hot."

He licked his lips, eyes on Bast's cock, watching the teasing movements. "I bet my mouth would feel even better."

"Mmm... yes." Bast arched, rocking strong and steady, red, wet tip appearing and disappearing in that pale fist.

He strained at the cuffs, cursing his stupidity at hiding the key in his ass where he couldn't get to it. If he'd been thinking, he would have put it in his hand and then he could have surprised Bast by suddenly being free, rolling his lover over and fucking him through... he groaned.

"Love you, Chosen." Bast's fist moved faster and faster still, snarls splitting the air, eyes flashing.

Trick's body reacted, cock growing harder, hips jerking. Oh, fuck, he wanted. "Bast..."

"Yes, Chosen? What do you need?" The motions were sibilant now, sliding and hot and full of hunger.

"You... feeding... something... anything."

Hot seed splashed over his chest and belly, Bast's eyes bright, face unbearably beautiful.

"Oh, fuck, I love you."

Trick wanted to reach up and trace Bast's features. He wanted to wipe his hand through the come on his chest and lick it off. He wanted to grab Bast's head and bring him down to feed. All he could do was watch, so that was what he did.

Bast leaned forward, licking and moaning at his neck, leather rubbing against his come-slick skin.

He let his head fall back, neck stretching. He could feel the key inside him, could feel Bast's ass against his cock, the tongue at his neck. "Please, baby-boy. Feed. Please."

The whisper that floated up to him a second before those teeth struck deep was a single word. "Mine."

He screamed, body shaking as he came, sinking into the pleasure that only Bast could give him. The pulls of pleasure washed over him, Bast's hands hard in his hair, keeping him still for Bast's bite.

It went on and on, eternity in living in Bast's need.

Finally Bast grew heavy, lax upon him, tongue sliding over his skin. "My love. My Chosen."

"Your Chosen," he whispered, feeling sated and heavy and so alive.

"Yes." Bast nuzzled close, hands wandering up to stroke his wrists. "The key, Sweets?"

He chuckled. "Hidden on my person."

Fingers slid around the cuffs, through his hair, Bast looking lazily, still languid and warm against him.

"You're cold, baby-boy. Very cold."

"Not true!" Bast lifted his head, eyes twinkling. "I'm full of you, Chosen. I'm never warmer than now."

He laughed, pushing his head up and stealing a kiss. Hot and wet and tinged with copper, Bast's tongue pressed deep, pushing his head back onto the pillow. Laughter turned to moans as his cock twitched and began to fill, Bast making him want again.

The kiss continued, stealing his breath as Bast's hands wandering, searching along his spine. He undulated beneath Bast, soft moans pushing into Bast's mouth.

Fingers slid down his cleft, stuttering as they found the ribbon attached to the key and his mouth was filled with a surprised laugh. "Oh! You *are* wicked!"

"I have a lot to live up to," he told his lover, eyes twinkling.

Bast slid down his body, slowly shedding clothes, tongue licking at him. "Do you know why we never play with the silver cuffs with Rose or Bael?"

He shook his head, legs spreading in anticipation.

Dark eyes flashed up at him. "Because I can't break those particular cuffs, Trick."

"Oh..." He shuddered.

The implication of that was... oh.

Bast didn't say anything, just nodded and nipped his hip hard, fingers sliding the key out of his body. He moaned, wanting, not the key back, but Bast inside him. Bast didn't make him wait long, fingers pushing inside him, two, then three in short order, building his need.

"Oh, fuck! Bast. God. Now."

"Fuck, yes." Bast surged above him, hands wrapping around the cuffs, cock sliding in deep, filling him completely. He shouted out, hips slamming up.

Hard and deep and fast -- Bast pushed them both, drove them until his breath was gone, his focus only on those bright eyes. He wrapped his legs around Bast's waist, holding on, flying high. Bast stretched, shaking, teeth sinking into his wrist below the cuffs. He screamed again, the sound low, coming from his belly. It was better this time; it always was when Bast was inside him, when sex and feeding got all tangled together.

This time, when that hot tongue sealed his skin, his wrists were released and he was drawn into Bast's arms and held. The soft sounds that surrounded him were familiar and comforting and rich -- Bast at his most private.

He slid his arms around Bast's waist, holding on and snuggling in close. "Love you, Bast."

"I know." Soft blankets were tugged over them both. "I love you, Chosen."

The games were fun, but in the end it was this that mattered. Him and Bast, together.

The dark head found its spot over his heart, arms and legs tangling around him as they did every morning, his baby-boy twining with him.

He couldn't tell where he ended and Bast began.

And that was the best game of all.

# Chapter Two

Trick grinned as he stepped out of the elevator to the sound of the shower going. Bast lived in there. It was cute.

It was also sexy as hell.

He stripped down and lay down on the bed, hands behind his head as he waited. His cock started to firm as he thought of his baby-boy coming out all clean and warm and damp. Bast sauntered into the room, singing something low and odd and foreign, toweling the long, long black hair.

"Mmm... Sweets."

"Hey, baby-boy. Nice shower?"

Dark eyes slid over him, Bast licking his lips. "Uh-huh. Nice."

"What soap did you use?" he asked, hand out to Bast.

"Hmm? Sandalwood and rose..." Bast stepped forward, nostrils flaring, a hunger glowing in the black eyes.

"Let me taste?"

"Taste?" Bast's hand slid into his, the slender body coming to straddle his waist.

"Yeah. My tongue, your skin? You know -- taste." He leaned up, licking at one of Bast's nipples.

"Mmm... I'm all for tasting." Bast purred like some wild cat, hand in his hair. "I like tasting."

He nodded and moved over to Bast's other nipple, taking his one in his mouth and sucking.

"Oh..." Bast arched, rubbing against him.

Trick wrapped his hands around Bast's waist and then slowly dragged them up, feeling up his baby-boy, moaning around the hard little nipple in his mouth.

"Sweets..." His hair was tugged and he was pulled in close.

He turned his head up, mutely begging for a kiss. Bast's mouth dropped on his, tongue pushing in deep, teeth dragging along his bottom lip. He whimpered, hips pushing up, hands digging in as he tried to pull Bast closer.

Bast licked a drop of blood off his lip, purring, eyes glowing. "Taste good, Chosen."

"Oh, Bast." His cock jerked, his blood singing in his veins from Bast's need. Chosen. It meant he belonged to Bast, meant he was made for the vampire. It meant he wasn't just a meal ticket; Bast needed him. "Taste more."

His mouth was nipped again, the jolt of pleasure too short, too fast, blood lapped away. He moaned, hands roaming over Bast's skin, their tongues tangling. Bast chuckled and broke the kiss, moving down to drag that tongue over his neck, teasing.

Throwing his head back, he gave Bast a bigger temptation. “Please, baby-boy.”

Lips traced the vein in his throat, nibbling. “Oh, Chosen... I can feel you.”

“Yes. My heart beats for you.”

“Yes.” Teeth sank into him, heat pouring over him in a rush.

The pleasure moved through him like fire, making him scream, making him come. For those precious moments Bast’s heart beat with his blood, and they were the same.

When it faded, Bast was curled on him, purring, licking his neck. He chuckled lazily, hand coming up to stroke Bast’s spine.

Bast purred. “Feel good, Sweets?”

“Oh, yeah.” He managed to drop a kiss onto Bast’s head. “Of course the plan *was* that I was going to lick you.”

“Mmm... I’ve got time, Sweets. Lots and lots of time.”

“Cool.”

He wrapped his arms around Bast and let himself drift off. He’d lick his lover all over later.

# Chapter Three

Bast had woken up alone, peckish, temperamental and fucking *cranky*.

He knew where Trick was. Trick had left a note. Hell, Trick *needed* sunshine sometimes. Needed friends. Needed to work.

He didn't give a shit, really, but he knew.

He'd tried to work, tried to read, tried to watch movies -- none of it helped. Finally, he did the only thing that would amuse him until Trick got home. He'd actually pulled all the paintings off the walls and moved the furniture into a huge pile by the bed and ordered the paint and new light fixtures by the time the elevator started squeaking.

"Fuck, Bast -- I wasn't gone that long."

"Hours." Bast refused to feel guilty. Trick *knew* he got bored and lonely. "I'm repainting everything purple.

The entire place. Even found purple fixtures."

"Hey, it's your money." Trick grinned at him, sauntering over slowly. The way his Sweets walked was so sexy, leading with the hips, shaggy blond hair falling around broad shoulders. "I'm not too sure what the landlord's going to say about it though."

It took him a second and then he got it, chuckling at his clever, clever lover. His lover who'd obviously forgotten that, while Trick might own the warehouse, Bast had the key to Trick's soul. "Oh, I think I can convince him."

"You do, do you? I'd like to know how -- I understand he's a real hard case."

Bast reached down, slid his hand over Trick's cock, rubbing. "I hope so, Sweets. In fact, I count on it." He pushed close to Trick, humming at the good, musky scents, the heat.

Trick chuckled, the sound low and sexy as fuck. "Fuck, you're hot."

"You're one to talk." He rocked against Trick's thigh, purring at the rush of sensation.

"You really going to paint the walls purple?" Trick asked, hands sliding down along his back to cup his ass.

"Well... I could be being a tad impulsive... I was bored." He stretched and pushed into Trick's hands. "And horny."

Trick laughed. "Being horny makes you want to redecorate? That's a new one."

He pouted, making sure it looked good. Redecorating was good for the soul. "I woke up and was lonely and bored and grouchy. I could go for grouchy again, you know."

"Oh, you think you can pull of grouchy with all this," Trick said, and pulled him tighter against that lean body, rubbing them together, "at your disposal?"

"Mmm... I could try. Being hungry makes me grouchy and all *this*," Bast purred and wrapped his arms around Trick's neck, one leg sliding up along a strong thigh. "Makes me hungry."

Trick's fingers slid along his crack, teasing his hole through the velvety material of his skin-tight pants. "Just how hungry are you?" Trick asked.

"Oh..." He leaned his head back, gasping and grinning. God, he loved when Trick played. Better than decorating any day. "Getting hungrier by the minute, Sweets."

"Then the only question that remains is what exactly are you hungry for?"

He caught Trick's eyes, allowing the edges of his hunger to show. "Everything you'll offer, Chosen."

A shudder went through Trick's body, a soft whimper pushing past his Sweets' lips. "That's everything I've got."

"You're all I need." Finished playing, he pulled Trick down into a kiss, lips parted and hungry.

Trick made a soft sound and kissed him hard, tongue invading.

Bast moaned, crawling up Trick's body until his legs were wrapped around the slim waist, holding on tight. "Sweets..."

"Fuck, Bast."

Trick stumbled toward the bed, dropping him down hard, coming down on top of him. He nipped at Trick's bottom lip on the bounce, sucking it into his mouth, teasing them both. Trick grinned at him and nipped his upper lip in retaliation. The laughter was warm, bubbling between them as he pulled at Trick's shirt, seeking skin. Trick pressed their hips tightly together and raised his upper body up enough to help him get the shirt off. Then Trick rolled them and his own was next as he lay on top of Trick's warm body.

"Mmm..." He purred, mouth trailing along Trick's collarbone as their skin meshed. "You feel good. Taste good, too." He took a nibble here, a lick there, grazing.

Trick arched and shivered and moaned under his touches, body hot, hands hotter as they slid over his ass. Oh, this was fun, dragging his fangs along Trick's skin. Letting the tip press against a peaked nipple. Drawing that sweet, hot blood right up to the surface.

"Oh fuck -- I thought you were hungry, baby-boy."

He groaned, hips rocking into Trick. "I am. Starving. Aching for you."

"Then why are you teasing?" Trick asked, eyes dark, a hunger he knew too well in them.

"Because it makes you hot. It makes me hot. It makes us hard." He reached down to unfasten Trick's jeans. "I want you in me when I feed."

Trick shuddered, hips jerking up against him. "Bast!"

Such a good boy, to remember his name.

"Not yet. In me. Fuck me first, sweet." He was panting, hurrying now. "Need you, Chosen."

Trick wriggled beneath him, helping him get rid of jeans and velour pants, his Sweets' hands shaking against his skin.

Finally they were naked, Trick's cock rubbing against his hole, their lips fastened as the passion built and flamed. Trick's hands were hard on his hips, holding him, pulling him down onto that thick heat. Biting his lower lip, Trick moaned and thrust up, pushing in the rest of the way with a hard jerk.

He cried out, entire body shuddering. The hunger, so close to the surface, bloomed. He could feel it stretching his face, loosening his body. He could see the echo of his eyes inside Trick's as he snarled. "Chosen. Now. Feed me."

Trick's whole body arched, cock shoving deeper. His Sweets' head fell back, Trick offering the long line of his throat for Bast's pleasure.

He growled down, licking once before he sank into Trick's flesh, filling himself with heat and richness and... Oh, Chosen!

Trick's blood filled his mouth, ran down his throat and filled his belly. Trick's scream rang through the air, ringing in his ears. He was filled and surrounded. All was Trick. His lifeblood. His Chosen.

He settled and fed, slow and long, humming. He stroked Trick's skin, shivering with pleasure. Trick's screams faded to whimpers, those hands holding tight to his hips, the beautiful body shuddering and jerking beneath him.

He closed the wound slowly, trailing his tongue along the fine skin, tasting the blood and salt and unique flavor of his sweet again and again, reluctant to let it go.

"Bast..." Trick's whisper barely had breath, let alone sound. "Love you."

"Yes." He lifted his face to take a long, slow kiss, their hearts pumping together in time. "I love you, my Sweets. My Trick. My Chosen."

"Mmm... yours." Trick licked at his lips and nuzzled close.

"Yes. Mine." He nodded, taking another kiss. "I forgot to ask how your day was before the whole purple wall thing came up."

Trick shrugged, the movement shifting the cock inside him. "It was all right -- not nearly as good as what came up when I got home."

Bast chuckled, nipping Trick's bottom lip, tickled all through. "No, no I can't see how it could be."

Smiling, Trick caught his mouth and pressed a kiss on him. "What about you, baby-boy? Still bored?"

"If I lie and say yes can we keep fucking?"

Trick laughed at that, cock slipping from his body. "If you can get me up again -- we can keep fucking."

He nipped Trick's bottom lip, Trick's jaw, Trick's ear. "I might be able to manage."

"It'll be fun to try, anyway, won't it?"

"More fun than repainting."

"But at least something should still be purple."

"Be good, Chosen, or I'll make sure something really turns purple." He chuckled. "Or worse, gets remodeled."

"You wouldn't dare!"

He grinned down into those beautiful eyes. "And risk your... architecture? Not a chance."

"I didn't think so," murmured Trick, pulling him down for another sweet kiss.

He melted into the kiss, hard cock rubbing against a sweet, warm belly. Oh, just perfect.

The redecorating could wait until the next time he was bored.

# Chapter Four

Trick ate the last of his steak hurriedly, leaving three twenties on the table. A sizeable tip, but the waitress had seen to it that he'd been served quickly and he was leaving without waiting for the bill.

He shoved his hands in his pockets and headed toward the warehouse. It had been three days since he'd left, ending an argument by simply walking out into the sunlight, where Bast couldn't follow. He'd holed up with an old friend, nursing his wounds with cheap scotch and second-hand smoke.

He wasn't even sure now what they'd been fighting about. He'd been grumbling about the bad offerings on TV, and Bast had snarled at him in reply. The next thing he knew they were yelling at each other and he'd left before it got more intense than that. He'd seen too many fights ending in fists being thrown; black eyes and rainbow colored bruises being the only accessory he could remember his mother wearing consistently.

He could remember his last words to Bast just fine though, clear as a bell. "Don't expect me back."

It had taken him two days to calm down and a half-day to get into a hotel, get sobered up, cleaned up. Then he'd found a steakhouse and eaten more red meat than anyone should at a single seating. But he was going to need it if he was going to feed his baby-boy.

For three days he'd lived with the pull, the need to feed Bast. It wasn't why he was going back, but it was a part of it.

As he took out his key to call up the elevator it occurred to him suddenly that Bast might not be there when he got downstairs. The last time they'd fought Bast had closed up shop and been on his way back to Europe. Of course it had taken Trick longer to go looking for him back then, but the argument hurt more this time, at least it had him.

He wasn't sure what he'd do if Bast wasn't there.

Trick took a deep breath as the elevator stopped and opened the grating, pushing the button for the basement. He was nearly bouncing in place by the time the elevator stopped, nerves making it impossible to stand still.

Taking another deep breath, he pulled up the grating and called out. "Bast?"

The apartment was dark, the television blinking eerily, some old horror movie playing without sound. The apartment was clean -- oddly so -- and it took him a moment to notice that a few lamps and one of the long sofas was missing, the marks from the furniture's heavy legs still in the carpet.

No one answered him, but there was a still, vaguely

Bast-sized lump on the bed, buried beneath the bunched covers. He worried his bottom lip, wondering what the missing furniture could signify then let it slip from his mind. He toed off his shoes and flung his leather jacket at a chair before making his way over to the bed.

"Bast?"

"If you came to get your clothes and stuff, take the fucking luggage with you. If you came to tell me to leave, then I'll need it." Bast's voice was tight, miserable, and he moved away from Trick with a soft, almost pained sound.

"I don't want anyone to leave, Bast." He sat on the edge of the bed and reached out, hand sliding over what he thought was Bast's shoulder. "I just had to get out before one of us started throwing punches."

"I've never hit you. I have never even threatened to."

"Yeah, I know." His voice was quiet, heavy. "It wasn't you I was worried about."

Bast snorted, voice flat. "If that's what you need, beat away. It's not like you can really damage me."

"No!" He shook his head and got up, pacing around the place as he tried to explain. "Do you know how many guys I saw my mom with? Guys who she said she loved, who said they loved her. And to a man they beat on her. Sooner or later they'd fight and yell and he'd start hitting her, hitting me, though most of the time it was just her.

"It doesn't matter if I can hurt you or not, I don't want to be one of those guys. And while we were yelling I could feel the urge to just reach out and smack you and I just had to go, had to get out before I did it." He stopped pacing and stared at the lump in the bed, willing Bast to understand. "I don't want to be one of those guys."

"What do you want, Trick? Why did you come

back?"

"I came back because I love you and I want to be with you. I just needed to calm down and not be so angry, not feel like hitting anyone." Trick frowned and went back to the bed, sitting on the edge. "Are you going to forgive me and tell me it's okay, or are you going to stay hiding under the blankets and hate me forever?"

"I'm going to stay hiding under the blankets and forgive you."

Trick smiled and began to strip. "Well that's all right then. I'll just have to come hide under the blankets with you."

"You sure there's room for you in here? I take up a lot of space." Bast didn't move, but the flatness was fading from his voice, becoming more alive, more familiar.

"Well... where I come from there's always room for the one who brings the eats." He slipped beneath the covers, pushing Bast over, trying to hide his shock at how cold Bast's skin felt. "And I can do that one better -- I am the eats."

"Sweets." Bast gave a soft sob. "I've missed you."

Wrapping his arms around the slender, naked body, Trick pulled Bast close. "Fuck, you're like a popsicle."

"Yeah, been sorta blah." Bast turned, face drawn and grey. "Where've you been?"

"Getting plastered, then sobering up and realizing the only thing I wanted in life was back here. You look like shit."

Trick pulled Bast's face to his neck. "Feed, baby-boy."

"Oh..." Bast shuddered, nuzzling desperately against his skin. Lips found his veins and then Bast shook his head and pulled back, eyes glowing at Trick. "Kiss me first. First we make up. Then I feed."

He was torn between doing as Bast asked and insisting on making his lover well. Then there was his own need, his blood was singing to him, demanding he feed Bast; he could feel the itch beneath his skin.

His mouth closed over Bast's, the vampire's lips slowly warming. Bast kissed him, tongue thrusting deep, blood-tinged tears streaking over the pale cheeks. Arms and legs wrapped around him, cold and clammy against his warmth.

He rolled them until Bast was beneath him. Whispering softly, "Sorry, so sorry," over and over again, he dropped soft kisses on Bast's face.

"Me, too. Yes. Need you, Sweets. Please, please, Trick." Bast was arching, sobbing and pressing up against him.

He shoved two fingers into Bast's mouth, straddling his lover now. "Suck."

The hungry lips fastened over his fingers, pulling hard, teeth scraping against his skin. Bast's eyes were glowing brightly, need obvious in the drawn face. He shuddered each time Bast's teeth moved against his flesh.

Finally tearing his fingers out of Bast's mouth, Trick rose to his knees and reached back, pushing them into his body.

"Hurry. Hungry for you, Trick, Sweets. Hurry."

He didn't take his time, didn't finesse or tease, just shoved his fingers up his own ass, stretching himself roughly. Seconds later he took them out and reached for Bast's cock, guiding it to his entrance.

Bast curled up, hands wrapping around Trick's shoulders, hips pushing up into him. "I want you. I missed you. I need you."

"I love you." He said the words as he sank down, eyes on Bast's.

"Yes." Bast's muscles bunched and suddenly he was spinning, Bast rolling them over and beginning to thrust inside him with long, deep motions. As Trick watched, Bast's face went feral, lips curling away from his fangs. "Hungry for you."

Moaning, he reached up, cutting his fingers on the teeth, feeling small jolts like electricity move through him. Bast's eyes widened, thrusts speeding, pushing deeper. A low growl filled the air, wild and hungry and feral. Trick arched into the thrusts, throwing his head back to expose his neck, eyes never leaving Bast's face. He could feel his pulse in his cock and in his neck, the blood pumping through him, surging, eager.

Quick, so quick Trick didn't even see him move, Bast struck, sinking his fangs deep within Trick's throat. He screamed as the pleasure whipped through him, driven by the long, sucking pulls at his neck. The world went crimson and then darker until it was black and all he knew was the beat of their hearts, his and Bast's, beating together.

Slowly, so slowly, Trick fell back into his body, Bast wrapped tight around him, murmuring softly, hands sliding over his skin. "Love you, Sweets. So much. Missed you, was so hungry and so lost."

"I love you, Bast. More than anything."

Bast was warm, lips pressing against his eyes, his cheeks, his mouth, loving him.

# Chapter Five

Oh, he was pissed.

He wasn't even completely sure *why* he was pissed.

Maybe it was the moon, or the time of year, or the fact that it was raining *again* and there wasn't much to do and the damned sun never seemed to go down these days.

And his pants were itchy.

He was on the way to call the dry cleaners to complain about his pants when he tripped on a stray electrical cord, sending himself, the phone, the alarm clock, a dozen books and a lamp crashing to the floor.

"God damn it!" The phone went careening against the wall.

"Motherfucking son of louse-ridden, three-legged, ulcerated whore!" The lamp shattered beautifully.

"Fucking bag of shit. Stupid cretinous evil lousy crappy frigging day!" The books weren't nearly as satisfying as the lamp.

Bast headed toward the kitchen for the plates.

The elevator began to groan, warning of Trick's immanent arrival.

"Oh, fuck me." Bast looked around the apartment at the mess.

The elevator was relentless, continuing to make its decent; it only ever broke down when it was inconvenient. He was still standing halfway to the kitchen when the grate opened, Trick strolling out, jacket hooked over one shoulder, hips leading.

Trick stopped as he saw the mess. "Well, fuck me."

"I fell. I'm cleaning it up. How're you?" Bast went to find the broom. He was relatively sure they had a broom.

Somewhere.

Trick followed after him. "You fell? How? Are you all right? What do you mean, you fell?" There was genuine worry in his lover's voice. "Did you hurt yourself? Are you all right?"

"I fell as in I tripped over all the fucking wires and I'm fine." Bast dug through the panty, tossing things about. "I'm just bitchy and in a bad mood and don't we have a fucking broom?"

Trick's arms slid around his waist from behind, warm breath sliding against the skin of his neck, followed by soft lips. "You mean a broom with a short handle for fucking?" Trick chuckled at his own joke and then stood back, grabbing his hand. He was led to a tall, thin cupboard next to the fridge and Trick opened the door, pulling out a broom. "Ta-da!"

"Show off." He grabbed the broom and headed to the mess, sweeping furiously. "Stupid glass and wires and fucking books, God damned silly elevator, never did like that stupid fucking, piece of shit alarm clock and these pants still itch!"

The broom was taking out of his hands, Trick efficiently sweeping everything into a corner, out of the way. "Take them off."

"What?" Bast stood in the middle of the floor, rant and reason for it taken away.

"Take the pants off." Trick set the broom against the wall and turned, one hand on his hip, the other hanging at his side. "Then they won't itch."

"Don't make sense, damn it. I'm *mad*. You'll ruin the whole snit if you make sense."

He resisted the urge to stomp his foot.

Trick shrugged. "Suit yourself; it just seems to me that if you're mad, you'd be better served slamming me up against the wall and fucking the shit out of me instead of complaining about your pants."

"I'm a pissed off vampire, not a horny old goat. Well, I am old and it's not that I don't want you, because I do, but... I want... well, I wanted to break all the plates, but you and that fucking elevator distracted me." Bast frowned as his voice developed an alarming shrill edge, and pulled off his pants, tearing them in half. "There. Stupid pants."

Trick looked as if he were fighting a grin as he slowly approached. "Do you want me to go get you the plates? Or do you want to tell me why you're so pissed off?"

"I don't know. I hate this time of year and I hate the rain and the sun and those pants and I'm just angry." He shook his head, frustrated beyond belief at the threatening tears. "You'd better get the plates."

Trick nodded, but he came closer, dropping a soft kiss on Bast's lips, warm hands sliding over his shoulders. "You sure I can't just distract you from it?"

Bast lifted his face for another kiss. "You can try."

Trick smiled and leaned down again, tracing his lips with the tip of that tongue. Hot hands roamed along Bast's back, finally sliding down to cup his bare ass at the same moment his tongue slipped in between Bast's lips.

"Oh." Lips opening, Bast wrapped his arms around Trick's shoulders, holding on tight. His Sweets was hot and strong and so alive beneath his hands.

"I know what the problem is," Trick whispered against his lips, nipping them gently. "It's been days since you fed from me, baby-boy. Well..." another kiss and more nibbling. "It's been a lot of hours anyway."

"Oh, Trick. Sweets." Bast closed his eyes, pressing close. He wanted Trick, needed him. "You sure it's not too soon?"

"I think it's been too long. Take me to bed, Bast. And *take* me."

"Yes." Bast buried his face in Trick's neck, teeth scraping sharp against the salt-sweet skin.

Slowly, he backed Trick toward the bed, hands pulling and tugging at Trick's clothing as they went.

Trick's fingers were busy at his shirt, undoing buttons and pulling it off. "Need you, baby-boy."

"Yes. Need you, love." He lifted his head long enough to pull Trick's t-shirt off. "Want to feel you, taste you."

Trick was working on his jeans, toeing off his shoes as he pulled down his zipper. He shimmied out of them, rubbing against Bast as he did so, cock hard and hot and insistent against Bast's belly.

Bast nipped sharply against Trick's throat at the touch, Trick's flavor teasing on his tongue, feeding his hunger. "Bed. Now. Hungry."

Trick moaned and flung himself back against the mattress, pulling Bast along with him. Long legs spread, cradling him. He burrowed into Trick's heat, whimpering as his mouth sought Trick's throat, searching for the sweet, heated splash of life that he needed more than anything.

Warm arms and legs wrapped around him as Trick's head fell back for him. "Please, baby-boy."

"Yes." He found the spot where they fit together and bit, sinking immediately into the calm, rhythmic truth of Trick's pulse. Better than sex or drugs or life or anything -- because he could feel Trick, nothing but his lover and it was so pure and sweet and addictive and his and he needed it more than anything.

Anything.

Trick had sobbed softly and came, body jerking against him. As he continued to suckle, Trick continued to cling, breath slowing, matching his own, the occasional shudder working its way through his lover's body.

He sucked as long as he dared, trying to fill himself with peace and then Bast reluctantly let Trick go, curling close around him. "I love you."

"Mm... me, too." Trick's words were slightly slurred, his hand sliding lazily along Bast's back.

Bast nuzzled that fine skin softly. "I don't know what I'll do, when I lose you." He sighed and closed his eyes.

Trick made a soft, distressed noise and clung to him. "Not going anywhere, baby-boy."

"Oh, good." He stroked Trick's belly softly, listening to the steady beat of his lover's heart.

It was a lie. He knew it. It was always a lie, because

they were always dying. But pretending that he believed in that particular lie was a finely-honed skill practiced on lovers and friends for centuries.

Everybody had a talent.

Trick kissed his arm, tongue lapping at him. "You feeling better?"

"Much. Thanks, Sweets." He curled close, stroking his chin against Trick. "We'll need to go buy a new lamp and alarm clock at some point, I guess."

"I bet you could find something cool on the 'net."

"Mmmhmm. Just have something delivered, you think?"

His eyes were caught by the painting Bryce, the only other man who he'd been close to, had done -- the blonde, the gravestones, the years of loss. "I'm thinking we need to decorate altogether. Stuff we both pick out."

Trick chuckled. "You tired of post-modern gothic already?"

"Well, I did gothic and then Victorian gothic, modern gothic, and pop goth. I've explored the culture." He closed his eyes, holding his lover close. "And this way, I can break the old plates."

"As long as you do it for fun and not because you're angry. I'll even throw a few around with you."

Bast nodded and chuckled. "Sounds like fun. So, you want a floral bedspread? Plaid?
Leopard print?"

Making Trick laugh like that was a good way to forget his bad mood.

# Chapter Six

Bast knew someone, one of his own, was there. Not in the apartment, maybe not even in the warehouse, but in his space, his territory. It made him itchy, made him angry, made him want to keep Trick in the safety of their home.

Of course, it also made him want to go hunting.

Bast tied his black hair back, growling softly. Centuries of trying to convince himself and the world that he was another guy with interesting eating habits and one hell of a sun allergy, and it all gets shot to hell because of fucking territory issues.

He threw on a pair of leather pants and a soft turtleneck, looking over at Trick, sprawled out on the bed, watching him dress. Bast *knew* Trick was safer here, but he didn't want his Sweets out of his sight, not with another out hunting on *his* streets.

If he could feel the other, then it could feel him.

"So what's up? You've been growling all day." Trick made a vague hand gesture at himself. "And, not that I mind getting fucked into oblivion, but it came on rather suddenly."

Bast looked over, eyes roaming over Trick with hunger. There were tiny pink bite marks ranging over the lean body, marks that another would know, marks that meant 'mine' and 'taken' and 'Chosen'. "I needed you, Sweets."

Trick smiled and one of his hands slid down along his body, fingers finding the marks as they went and stroking across them. "Come back to bed, baby-boy. I don't feel like going out."

"I need to..." His voice trailed off, attention split. Trick's body smelled so good, warmth mixed with need and musk and blood and come...

He wasn't hungry, not at all. He shouldn't even be hard, not after the past forty-eight hours or so, but the constant irritation of the other stripped him down to lower layers of need. Trick was his Chosen, his love, his heartbeat and, although he knew it was unlikely anyone would come for Trick, his gut insisted that someone was coming, someone wanted to steal the sweetness and joy and *life* that was his Trick. Just the thought sent him growling the bed, hands sliding over muscled legs.

"Sweets."

Arching lazily up into his touch, Trick purred.

He bent forward, nuzzling at Trick's balls, breathing in his lover, hands sliding up to touch each mark reverently. "I need to go out. I have someone I should see... Fuck, you smell good, Sweets..."

Trick's legs came up, knees bracketing his head and

warm hands slid over his own. "You sure about that? If you really want to go out, I can be dressed in a few minutes, but..." Trick's hips pushed toward him, "I'd rather stay here where we don't need clothes."

"Mm... yes. No clothes... want you." He laved the heavy sacs slowly, sucking tiny pieces of skin into his lips again and again. His cheek rubbed against the softness of Trick's inner thigh.

Soft whimpers filled the air, Trick's hands clutching at his. "You make me feel so fucking good."

"Good. ." Bast's tongue continued up, sliding along the thick base of Trick's cock, rubbing the shaft with the length of his fangs, letting Trick feel the threat and promise of his bite.

Trick moaned and jerked slightly, hands moving up along his arms to find his head and sliding into his hair. "I love you, Bast." Trick's voice was throaty and rich.

Bast sobbed, body and mind and heart aching with something so much more than pleasure. He moved to lick at the tip of Trick's cock, lapping at the clear drops that were gathering. When those were gone, Bast wrapped his lips around the swollen head and began pulling, needing more.

Trick curled around him, belly warm against his head. After several sucks, Trick lay back again, hips moving now. He could stay here for hours, Trick's cock sliding over his tongue, filling his mouth and throat. Bast closed his eyes, losing himself into the rhythm of Trick's heartbeat, Trick's moans, Trick's thrusts.

Trick began stroking his hair, trying to draw his attention. "Gonna take awhile," he warned.

Bast hummed softly, shifting his body so that he could press close, cheek settling on Trick's belly. Warm, satisfied pleasure filled him, the sounds of Trick's body comforting him. His Chosen, his Sweets, his lover, his Trick.

Something rattled suddenly against the base of his spine, an electricity that wouldn't be ignored and Bast lifted his head with a snarl.

They had found him.

"Bast? What the fuck?" Trick was blinking down at him, cock pressing urgently against his chin, the hand in his hair trying to encourage him back to the eager erection.

"Someone's here. Into the bathroom, Trick, and stay there until I come for you." Bast moved off the bed, his low growl filling the air as he stalked toward the elevator. "Move, Sweets. Now."

"What?" Trick got up and wrapped a sheet around himself. "Who's here? I want to help you."

"Get in the bathroom, Trick. Stay safe for me, just until I know who it is." Bast looked over as he stepped into the elevator. "You're mine. You're safe in here, but not upstairs, you understand? Not upstairs. If I don't come back down, you're safe in here."

He stepped into the elevator and shut the grate, mind focused on the interloper.

"If you don't come back?" Trick made a dash for the elevator, rattling at the grate, but his strength was no match for Bast's. "What the hell is going on? Bast? I don't want to be safe if you don't come back."

"I love you, Sweets. Go lock yourself in the bathroom and wait for me." Bast made himself smile at Trick and then start the elevator.

"Fuck you -- don't do this to me -- don't leave me behind like some little kid, let me help you!" He could hear Trick banging on the grate above the groan of the elevator. The noise stopped abruptly and Trick's voice floated up to him. "Come back to me, baby-boy."

"I will, Chosen." The whisper was lost to the grind of gears and Bast let his hold on humanity slip away, eyes bright and hot, mind speeding, liquid fire filling his still veins.

When the elevator doors opened, Bast snarled. "Whoever you are, you are intruding upon claimed ground. I give you one opportunity to remove yourself from my home. This is not a Haven for our kind."

The boy that stood in the corridor, for he indeed was a boy, both in appearance and in years, turned as he spoke. He was dressed in black, jeans and leather jacket dark against pale skin. His hair was blond, his eyes washed out blue and he stood, hips leading, a sardonic smile on his face. He reminded Bast enough if Trick that it hurt.

"Remove myself?" The intruder laughed. "Or what?" The voice wasn't Trick's at all.

"Or I will remove you myself." Bast tilted his head. "Are the customs so slack that children are let loose upon the world with no manners?

The boy shrugged, looking patently unconcerned. "Things change, man. The new generation turns the older one away, makes its own rules. You're an Apostolos, right? Been around for awhile. Maybe too long."

"Are you challenging me, boy? For fuck's sake, you've got an entire goddamned hemisphere with *maybe* a dozen of us around. Go west, young man, and stake your claim." Bast's eyebrows felt like they had met his hairline. A challenge? Now? Here? In this day and age?

He hadn't met a challenge in over hundred years, had lived happily away from the strongholds and Havens in the New World and this *child* was going to try to screw things up after he'd found Trick?

Fuck. He didn't think so.

"You're the one with the problem, man." The boy shrugged again. "This is a great place to find food without having to chase it down. Easy enough to cover things up if you go too far, too, you know?" The other vampire laughed, like it was a problem he was familiar with. "I'm not asking you to leave, but I'm not going anywhere either."

"No, child, I wouldn't know." Bast snarled, stepping forward, fangs bared. "I do not make it a practice to foul my house. I do not take from the unwilling and I do not relinquish my claim to this place. Why are you here?"

The boy sneered, exposing his own fangs. "I told you -- the hunting's good. Rumor had it you were one of the fun ones despite your age. Rumor was obviously wrong. I didn't come to fight, but I don't mind if I have to."

"I am not seeking a fight. This is *my* home and you were not invited. You do not introduce yourself, you do not come in friendship, you prey upon my flock. If you wish to survive, then learn to follow the fucking rules." Bast shook his head, eyes flaring at the thought of Trick waiting for him downstairs. "If you wish to talk, I will meet you elsewhere, but this place is mine and there is no place for you."

Another snort and the boy crossed his arms. "I'm not going anywhere, old man."

"This is your last warning, child. I will defend my home." *And my Chosen.*

The intruder's eyes flared bright orange, his fangs bared on a snarl as he leapt at Bast. Bast met the attack instinctively, his eyes flashing. The first blow caught his cheek, but the second blow was his, battering the younger vampire's midsection and then he leapt close to deliver a deep bite to a leather covered shoulder.

A scream met his bite, sharp blows flailing against his shoulders and his head. Bast took each blow, mouth tearing into soft flesh, holding on like a dog, jaw clamped tight. The taste of dead blood in his mouth was vile, rotten and spoiled and unwilling and wrong.

They struggled violently, the blows to his head and neck making him dizzy. The boy kicked at his legs, sending him down, but he refused to relinquish his hold on the boy's shoulder and they went down together. They rolled, the other vampire pushing at his head now, trying to make him stop, make him let go as the blood poured from the wound.

Bast waited and finally the boy made a fatal mistake in his panic, head rolling back as he shoved and fought. With a move as instinctive as it was practiced, Bast's fangs found the jugular and tore it open. The hands battering at him grew quickly weaker, one going to the boy's neck, trying to hold the wound closed. The other vampire started making strangled, choking noises, body going still and quiet beneath Bast.

Bast groaned, body shuddering violently, heaving as he knelt upon the dusty floor, taste of death upon his tongue.

Finally he managed to stand, head spinning violently. Dawn was coming. Dawn was coming and he had a dead body to deal with. As quickly as his shaking hands could manage, he stripped the vampire and threw the blood spattered clothes into a trash bag. Then he pulled a metal barrel in front of the window, throwing the naked body within.

He'd cleaned up the floor and dragged another barrel

over to cover the newly cleaned spot by the time the sun hit the barrel. The body burned quickly, leaving nothing but a faint stench. The clothes he'd send back to whoever claimed the boy.

Finally, he stumbled into the elevator and closed the grate, pressing the button for home.

As soon as the elevator stopped, the grating was thrown open.

"Fucking shit! Are you okay?" Before he could answer, Trick was on him, dragging him out of the elevator and slamming him up against the wall. "Are you fucking okay?"

"Shower. Need a shower." Bast shook his head. "Gotta get the smell off me." He hurt, from head to toe, and he knew he owed Trick an explanation -- something. But not now. Not right now. Now he needed to be naked and in his shower getting the smell of death off his skin.

Trick was shaking his head and he looked dangerously near tears. "You've got blood all over you -- you tell me you're okay, damn it!"

"I'm a little bruised, Sweets. Blood's not mine. Gonna be okay, promise." Bast slumped against the wall. "Need to get clean, Trick. Please."

Trick glared at him for a moment longer. "You owe me an explanation." He waited until Bast nodded and then picked Bast up, hoisting him up over his shoulder and heading for the bathroom.

Bast kept his eyes closed, the sensations of moving and hurting enough to make him more than a little nauseated. He wanted to be cleaned and warm and held close -- although as pissed as Trick was, it may be a bit before he'd have the last.

He was let down and stripped and put in the shower,

Trick leaning past him to turn on the taps, the water almost, but not quite, too hot. Bast arched, letting the heat soothe his bruises. Carefully -- not thinking, not remembering, not doing anything but reaching for the soap and scrubbing again and again -- he cleaned himself.

He could feel the weight of Trick's gaze, knew his Sweets was watching him, unblinking and solemn. Suddenly the scent of his shampoo bloomed and Trick's hands were in his hair, working the soap in, making lather. The familiar fingers were massaging his scalp, fingernails scrapping with exactly the force he liked.

"Sweets. I love you." He sighed, head falling back, relaxing beneath the touch, adrenaline fading away.

Trick's lips pressed hard against his and then he was being pushed under the spray. Trick rinsed out his hair and then the rest of him, hands sliding over his skin, helping the water sluice away the soap. Fingers lingering over bruises that would be fading already, Trick never made a sound.

"What do you want to know, Sweets?"

"Everything." Trick's voice was hard, but vulnerable at the same time.

"It was another of my kind, a young one, newly made, poorly raised. He wouldn't play by the rules. He wanted to hunt here. I refused, we fought, he died." Bast sighed, tremors shaking him slightly.

"Fucking shit!" Trick's arms wrapped around him like tight bands. "You should have told me where you were going."

"I didn't know who it was; just that it was another vampire." He leaned into Trick's solid body. "I needed to know you were safe."

"What if you didn't beat him?"

"He couldn't have come down and this all belongs to you. I need to make you a plan -- people you can call and shit." Bast shook his head. "I never thought anyone would come. No one's hassled me in two hundred years."

"No, I mean... Fuck, Bast." Without warning Trick's mouth covered his, hard with anger and fear and relief and need. He was shoved against the wall again, Trick's body landing hard and heavy against him.

Bast pressed up against Trick, lips parting beneath that panicked need. He knew this, knew all about fear and shock and hunger. He could've lost Trick, lost his lover to a sorry bag of flesh who only wanted blood. Wanted his territory. His home.

Trick grabbed his hands, bringing them up over his head, holding them both there with one hand as the other wandered along his body, fingernails scraping, fingers tugging, pushing, bruising. Trick's foot kicked his legs apart, his cock was hard and hot and insistent against Bast's belly. The water splashed around them, making them move slickly together.

"Sweets..." He didn't fight Trick, letting his lover touch and mark and move him. "My Trick."

His Sweets' mouth closed over his neck, near his jugular, biting hard, teeth breaking the skin and then scraping along the skin down to his collarbone. Bast's cry bounced off the tile, mixing with the hot water, and he arched up toward Trick's mouth.

Trick's free hand moved to his buttocks, lifting him, tilting him until he could feel Trick's cock, hot and urgent, pressing against him.

"Yes. Fuck, please, love. Please." Bast's hips moved restlessly, hunger and need making him ache.

Trick let him drop, cock slamming up into his body as

he fell on it. Trick's hand moved to his hip, holding him tight enough to bruise, pulling his body up, away and then guiding him back down onto the thrusting card. The hand around his wrists tightened, helping Trick pull him up, keeping him suspended between Trick's hand and the thrusting cock, the hot mouth and sharp teeth in between, biting and scraping at his shoulder, his collarbone, his neck.

Bast was flying, sobbing, calling out his need and hunger as Trick fucked him, took him, loved him. Time stopped, the world stopped, everything stilled but the teeth on his skin and the cock slamming into his body.

Harder and faster, deeper, Trick fucked him and marked him and filled him. Finally Trick raised his head, exposing his own neck. "Take me."

He came when his teeth pierced Trick's throat, seed pumping from his cock as sweet blood poured into his lips. Trick's scream filled the air, hot seed pulsing into him like the blood that pumped down his throat. He fed, pulling against Trick's throat as they sank together to the floor of the shower, drinking deeply. He made it last as long as possible, slowly closing the wound, licking wet, salty skin.

Trick was shaking against him, soft sobs heaving against his chest, the strong arms wrapped around him, hands clutching.

Bast wrapped around him, fingers stroking over his back, murmuring softly. "Sweets, I won't let anyone hurt you. You're mine -- my heartbeat, my Chosen. I love you."

"I love you. I love you." Trick's mouth searched blindly for his own.

The kiss was flavored by tears and Bast drank Trick

in, holding him close, petting and purring. When Trick was relaxed in his arms, Bast freed his lips, brushing soft kisses over his cheeks. "My Sweets."

Trick huddled against him, quiet and warm beneath his hands and the spray of the water.

"Talk to me, Sweets? How can I make this better?" Bast nuzzled and kissed, worry making him ache. "What can I do?"

"I've always thought you were going to live forever."

"Well, I know some of my kind who have lived for millennia, but we can die, Sweets. Everything can die. We're only animals."

"I know, I just..." Trick looked at him, blue eyes large in a face more vulnerable than Bast could ever remember seeing it. "I never thought you would before I did. I've counted on feeding you until the day *I* die." Trick's hands opened and closed and his voice dropped to a whisper. "I don't think I can live without it anymore, Bast."

"Oh, Sweets." Bast took another kiss, caressing his Chosen with trembling hands. "I won't leave you here alone, Trick. I have never lost a challenge and I have you to protect. You are my heartbeat. I will be there holding you close when you leave this life."

"I love you." A great, shuddering sigh shook Trick and then he pushed himself up to his knees and turned off the water before reaching over and grabbing one of the large towels. "Take me to bed and make love to me?"

"Always." Bast stood and took the towel from Trick, wrapping him in the softness. "Come let me love you."

# Chapter Seven

Bast was screaming at his sister on the phone.

In Greek.

It was one of his favorite things to do -- to get her utterly infuriated and screeching and then have a nice, violent, long-distance row.

Sometimes he even threw things.

It wasn't that he didn't love her -- although, to be honest, he'd only seen her twice in the last century and that was two times too many -- it was just that she was so stodgy and uptight and boring. Cecilia needed a good fight to blow the cobwebs loose once every decade or so.

So, today was the day. She'd sent him an invitation to her wedding -- her four hundred and eighth, to be exact, little money-grubbing whore Brykolos, he was *so* proud -- to some child who would worship at her perfectly manicured feet and beg her to turn him for twenty years before that bored her. Bast'd called to refuse the invitation.

After all, he did *know* how the silly ceremonies went.

She'd cried and screamed and called him a reprobate and sixty or seventy other well-loved terms before the real fun started. They were heading into the breaking of things when the elevator grate opened.

"Fucking shit, Bast! What the hell is going on? I could hear you down the street!" Trick looked concerned, the frown making lines appear on his forehead and between his brows.

Bast screamed another volley of insults into the phone and then covered the mouthpiece with his hand. "My sister."

A half smile quirked his sweet's face, making the lines disappear. "I take it you aren't close."

"Not at all, thank goodness." He fired off another shot, making sure to comment on her body odor and general resemblance to a breed of ill-tempered hairy goat.

Trick shrugged out of his jacket and let it drop over the back of the lounge chair. He threw himself down on the bed, leaning up on one elbow to watch. "Do I get translations, or do I have to guess from the expressions on your face?"

"Oh, I like the idea of guessing, Sweets. You look good, by the way." He smiled, then explained to Cecilia that she was quite possibly less intelligent than a rotting sea sponge.

"What's the topic under discussion? And thank you." Trick preened a little and pushed his hand beneath his t-shirt to scratch at his belly. When he was done, the t-shirt had pulled up on the one side, showing just a hint of the warm skin.

"She's getting married again and expects an audience." His next insult was half-hearted, distracted as he was by Trick's skin. He wandered over to stand by the bed, stroking it with one finger.

"I'm surprised you're not eager to go -- you like a good party." Trick smiled at him and lay back on the bed, hands behind his head. It pulled the black t-shirt up another couple of inches.

"Shitty party. *Very* boring. Stuffy." He leaned over to drop a kiss on that sweet skin, nuzzling gently.

The phone was set on the bed, his sister's voice a distant squeal.

Trick laughed, propping himself back up on both elbows, which made the muscles of his stomach contract in the most lovely way. "Isn't she going to know?"

"Know what?" His tongue traced along one side of Trick's navel, lapping up the hint of salt.

Trick moaned and his stomach muscles clenched tighter. "That you're not... oh... listening."

"Oh, who the fuck cares." He reached out and pushed the phone off the bed, pushing Trick's t-shirt up a bit higher. "She'll live."

That made Trick laugh and he lay back again, pushing his stomach up toward Bast's mouth. "If you make me scream -- a lot -- then she'll hear, and she'll know you're having sex, or killing someone I suppose, instead of listening to her..."

"Mmm... that'll really piss her off and get the two of us laid in the process. Excellent plan, Sweets." He began to nibble, sharp little bites along Trick's skin that he immediately eased, teasing and arousing.

Trick moaned loudly, pushing into the bites and licks. "I only ever have... I have... have... oh fuck it -- don't stop, baby-boy."

He had no intention of stopping, not now that he had Trick's flavor on his tongue. He moved up, pushing the shirt as he went, uncovered the tight nipples. With a grin, he snagged the little bud of flesh with a fang, then suckled, pulling fiercely for only a moment before closing the wound. Not enough to push either of them over the edge, but enough to drive them both mad, he repeated the actions again and again.

Trick's hands were in his hair, twisting and holding him tight. There was a hard, hot bulge in the black jeans, Trick pushing up and rubbing against his legs with short, desperate movements.

He lifted up to look, eyes hot in his head. "Want to fuck you when I feed, Sweets."

"Oh fuck!" Trick jerked against him, finger's tightening in his hair. "Yes. Fuck yes."

He surged up, heat and hunger and ferocity filling him, fangs resting against Trick's neck. "Lose the pants and get the fucking lube, love. I'm *hungry*."

"Shit!" Trick's hands slid between them, fingers ripping at his button and pulling down the zipper. Then he began to wriggle, working the tight jeans off, eyes never leaving Bast's.

His own fingers were doing the same, pushing the slacks down over his hips, body hot and hard and so hungry, so very... "Hurry, Trick." His fangs just pierced the skin, the scent of the fresh blood a tease.

Trick jerked again, feet kicking the jeans away. "Fuck! Screw the lube, baby-boy, just do it."

He reached down, smearing the head of his cock with

the drops of precome that formed there. Then he pressed against Trick's entrance, pushing inside as his teeth sank into Trick's throat.

Sweets screamed for him, loud and long, body pushing into both invasions, pulling him in deeply and flooding into him at the same time. Wild pleasure, so erotic, so necessary, so huge, drove him into Trick's body, mouth pulling as his hips pushed. His hands were tight upon his that lean body, tugging the beloved form closer, farther, nearer.

Trick own hands were like bands around his arms, holding on as his Sweets jerked between the sensations, still screaming softly, loudly, fading, rising.

He climax hit him hard, tongue sliding across the wound to close it just before he began to jerk in pleasure.

Trick whimpered beneath him, hands holding on like that was all that was keeping Trick together. "Fuck, if that's what happens when you talk to your sister, I'm setting her number on autodial."

# Chapter Eight

Hungry.

He was hungry, could feel it curling up his belly, into his chest, making his jaw tight.

Trick was gone, some nonsense about his mother and brother and a wedding. He hadn't been exceptionally excited about going, but it had only been a week and Bast thought maybe Trick wanted to make his appearance, show them he was happy and settled and independent.

At this point it didn't really matter. A week was a week was a week was seven whole days without eating and he was hungry.

He paced restlessly, fingers itching to reach for the phone, call Trick's cell, find out if he was at the airport, in the taxi, in the elevator.

The familiar groaning of the elevator warned him someone was on their way down. If it was Rose or Bael, he was going to commit murder; it had to be Trick, he needed it to be Trick.

He snarled, furious at the snail's pace of the fucking piece of shit elevator, bouncing on the balls of his feet. It finally settled, the doors beginning to open and he stepped forward. "Sweets? Trick? 's it you?"

"Oh, baby-boy, I was worried I'd forgotten what you looked like." Trick looked tired, but those blue eyes lit up as they landed on him.

"Oh, Trick." Bast could smell Trick, it made his balls ache, his stomach clench.

He wanted and needed and hungered and had for days and now his heartbeat, his Chosen, was home. He looked up, his hunger a living thing, moving through his bones. "Home. You're home, love."

Trick's expression softened and he smiled. "I like it when you do that."

"Do? Do what?" He reached out to slide one finger against Trick's chest, the t-shirt soft and warm.

"Forget yourself and call me love." Trick laughed and shrugged. "Hey, I was just at a wedding; the place was oozing with sentimentality."

"Mmm..." Bast had made as much small talk as he could without feeling Trick's heat, so he pushed Trick's baggage out of the way and wrapped his arms around Trick, rubbing himself against the hard body, nose and lips and tongue exploring the delicious, hot, smooth line of throat.

Trick's arms came around him, his Sweets' head tilting back, giving him full access. "Missed you. Missed this. Thought I was going to go insane."

"So hungry. Haven't fed in so long... need you, Sweets." He was purring, rubbing and clutching, teeth sliding roughly along Trick's skin. "Hungry for you."

Trick's voice was a whisper. "What are you waiting for?"

He bit down in answer, sobbing as Trick's blood filled his mouth, splashing inside his empty body. Trick called his name, body shaking, heat spreading between them, hand clutching tightly to him.

Bast fed, pulling deeply, vision awash in red, body thrumming with energy. He had to force himself not to continue, not to feed and feed until his body, which screamed with worry that it was *starving*, quieted. Instead Bast healed the wound, still shaking as his tongue searched for the remnants of Trick's blood.

Trick was limp in his arms, eyes fluttering, pulse slow but even beneath his tongue. "Oh... needed that."

"Yes. Yes, Sweets." He was still nuzzling, moaning as he nipped and nuzzled. "Needed you."

Trick's hands were soft and gentle as they came up and moved over his face, fingertips tracing his features, sliding along his teeth last, caressing his incisors. Pushing hard against the sharp tooth, Trick pierced the skin of his thumb and pushed it into Bast's mouth.

"Oh..." He suckled with a happy purr, half walking, half carrying Trick over to the bed.

"I took steak to eat on the plane. And steak at the wedding. And I had a steak before getting on the plane." Trick continued to caress him with the fingers of his free hand, stroking through his hair. "Are you all right?"

Bast nodded, licking the pad of Trick's thumb. "Just hungry. Hadn't eaten. Needed you."

"At all? There was plenty of blood in the fridge when I left! I know -- I stocked it myself." Trick's forehead had those three little lines in it that always appeared when he was worried.

"I didn't need it, at first, and then I didn't want it and then you were home soon and so I waited."

The lines grew deeper. "What if you hadn't made it? What if my plane was delayed or I got stuck in traffic or-"

Trick pulled the finger out of Bast's mouth and wrapped both hands around his skull, pulling him down once again to the long neck. "Take what you need, baby-boy. Make yourself strong."

Bast sobbed, licking and nibbling on the sweet skin. "Just ate, Sweets. Should wait. Wanna make love. Wanna hold you. My Chosen, so good. Feels good."

"Are you sure you're okay, that you took enough?" Trick's blue eyes were serious, so full of worry. And love.

Bast answered him with a kiss, tongue thrusting with a steady beat that matched the rocking of his hips. Moaning, Trick pushed up into him, meeting each thrust with one of his own.

"Yes, want you." Bast tore open Trick's shirt, hand sliding down the muscled stomach, scratching lightly.

Trick shuddered beneath his touch, so responsive to him, as if he were an instrument and Bast a master musician.

He bent down, nipping and dragging he teeth along exposed skin. His cock ached as he slid down, pushing against Trick's hip, Trick's thigh. His lover's fingers were twisting through his hair, sliding over his scalp and his face as if relearning the feel of them. Soft sounds of need and pleasure, sounds far too long absent, filled the air.

He licked his way down Trick's belly, humming happily at the flavors of salt and skin.

"Love you." Trick's hands tightened in his hair. "Love

you, Sebastian."

"Trick. Sweets." He nuzzled, fingers working open those black jeans.

"Oh, fuck yes. Touch me, please, touch me." Trick's hips were pushing up against his hands. "Never fucking leaving again."

"Promise?" Bast's fingers wrapped around Trick's cock, pumping as his tongue lapped at the tip.

"Never," Trick repeated, making it sound like a vow.

"Good." He took the head of Trick's cock into his mouth, sucking gently. So good -- salty, sweet, Trick... A gentle shudder ran through the lean body.

He settled close, eyelids falling closed as he purred and pulled, lips and tongue working the hot flesh. Trick's moans were like music and his hips were restless, pushing up, shifting, searching for more. Bast hummed happily, hunger quieted with his Chosen close and hot and sliding in and out of his throat.

The hands in his hair tightened again, this time with intent, holding him still as Trick's hips found a rhythm and began to ride it. Oh, so good, so right, Trick fucking his lips steadily, Trick's salt on his tongue, the sweet beneath him.

"Oh, fuck! Gonna come..." Trick's hips began to jerk, losing their grace as his lover lost control.

Bast swallowed, purring happily at the salt and need flavor of his Sweets. He didn't release Trick's shaft, just gentled his lips and tongue.

Trick lay quiet, almost purring, beneath him, just his fingers moving, carding slowly through Bast's hair. He let the soft, sweet flesh slide free, sliding up Trick's body and taking a slow kiss. Trick took a deep breath and joined their mouths together again.

Bast curled in tight, hunger and love and longing keeping him close, hands moving slowly.

"Naked," Trick murmured as his hands pushed at Bast's clothes. "One of us is wearing too many clothes and I'm pretty sure it isn't me."

Bast slid and wiggled out of shirt and slacks, moaning softly as he was pulled back into Trick's arm, against all that smooth skin. "That's better." Trick's hands began to wander over his body, exploring as if for the first time. "Fuck, I've missed you."

"Yeah, I missed you, Sweets." Bast purred and shifted, hand petting Trick's stomach. "Was the wedding cool?"

Trick shrugged, his belly moving beneath Bast's hand. "I never thought I'd see Mom marry anyone, but Derek says this guy is good to her -- he doesn't hit her or yell at her and he's got money and a really nice place up in New Hampshire." Another shrug, this one casual. "Derek's moved out there, mooching I bet, but I let them know I wasn't going to be coming out for handouts or anything."

Bast nodded, circling Trick's navel with a finger. "I missed you while you were gone."

"Yeah, baby-boy, I know. I was itchy the whole time and after about the third day it felt like I was gonna explode, like my veins were too full."

Bast nodded, fingers moving to card through the soft curls that crowned Trick's cock. "I was hungry, but I missed this most. Relaxing with you, playing with you." He leaned forward and dropped a quick kiss to Trick's nipple. "You're my best friend, Sweets. I missed talking to you."

Trick was quiet for awhile and then he spoke, voice thick. "You make me whole, make me believe in sappy romantic stuff I always thought was crap."

He nuzzled, humming softly with pleasure. He knew Trick loved him, knew it without a shadow of a doubt, but it still felt good to hear. "Mm… Sweets. I think we may have to stay like this for at least a month to recover."

"Only a month? I was hoping for two at the very least."

"Oh, I can live with that. Maybe three, just to make sure." Bast chuckled, nipping playfully at the skin beneath his lips.

Trick arched and chuckled and his hands stroked over Bast's skin. "Give me a bit and I'll be ready for more of that."

"I can wait. I just want to be close to you." Bast undulated between Trick's hands and body, loving the sensations that poured through him.

"There's nothing like the feeling of your skin. It's like silk, only warm, alive, moving. Do they make silk in liquid? That's what your skin would feel like."

"Mm… flattery will get you anywhere, Sweets."

Trick chuckled. "I don't think I even need the flattery. You're pretty much a sure thing."

"Pretty much? No, Sweets, you've had me lock, stock and barrel for a long time." He grinned and pressed up for a kiss. This was what he had missed. Loving Trick. Being close and warm and happy.

Trick looped an arm around his neck, keeping him in place. "Are you telling me you're easy?"

He nodded immediately. "Absolutely."

Trick's grin was wide. "Awesome." He was pulled down into a warm, sloppy kiss.

Bast chuckled into the kiss, hands sliding over Trick's throat and teasing at the faint scars. Trick made a soft, happy noise and his hips pushed up into Bast, cock filling between them.

"Love you." So responsive and seductive and sweet and his and... fuck, he was besotted. Bast grinned, nipping softly at Trick's bottom lip and making Trick groan.

He wouldn't have it any other way.

So good. Right. His Chosen. Home.

# Chapter Nine

Trick got off the elevator and looked around for Bast. There was no sign of his own, personal vampire, but as he tossed his jacket over the back of a chair he heard the sound of water running in the bathroom.

It made him laugh. Bast was cleaner than anyone he knew; his lover didn't even sweat. But he spent a quarter of his life in the shower.

It was a good thing Trick liked water, liked fucking in the strong, hot spray.

He shucked off his t-shirt and shimmied out of his jeans and opened the door into the steam-filled room. "You in here somewhere, baby-boy?"

"Mm... Sweets." Bast's voice was sex and need and hunger and desire and pleasure all mingled together in husky tones. "I was just thinking about you."

Through the fog he could see Bast's form, dark hair plastered to his shoulders, slender body writhing as Bast fucked himself slowly on dark dildo.

Trick moaned softly, hard in an instant. "You started without me..."

"Just warming up, Sweets. Giving you some encouragement." Bast moaned as the toy slid deep, cock full and heavy. "Oh, God. Touch me."

Trick didn't need to be asked twice. Stepping into the shower, he slid to his knees, hands starting at Bast's shoulders and dragging down along his chest and belly. He wrapped his fingers around prominent hips as his mouth swallowed Bast down.

"Fuck, yes!" Bast shuddered, his body shuddering violently. "Oh, Trick..."

He hummed happily, sucking vigorously. He slid his hands around to Bast's ass, fingers sliding over to touch the dildo as Bast played with it. The room filled with dark, hungry cries, Bast growling desperately as he thrust between Trick's mouth and the hard dildo. Bracing his knees against the sides of the stall, he sucked harder, pushing his thumbs into that tight ass along with the dildo.

Bast's scream heralded the splash of seed against the back of his throat, his lover shuddering violently, body spasming around his thumbs. He swallowed the bitter fluid eagerly, sucking the softening flesh until the dildo slid out of Bast's body, his thumbs still buried inside the warm hole.

"Oh... oh, Sweets. So good, so... oh, fuck. Need you."

He let the flaccid cock slide from between his lips, pressing a last kiss to it before turning his attention to the ribbed abdomen. He licked at the water that flowed over Bast's skin, moving his thumbs in small circles inside Bast's body.

"Mmm..." Bast was purring softly, body undulating lazily for him. "My Trick. Love you. Feels like magic."

"Have you any idea how incredible you look?" He whispered the words against Bast's skin. "You make me so fucking hard."

"Oh, good. If you're hard, that means you can fuck me when I feed." Bast's hands stroked his cheek softly. "I'm so hungry for you, Sweets."

A shudder went through him and he surged to his feet, shoving Bast up against the wall. His mouth closed over his lover's as he ground against the lean body. Bast nipped at his tongue, making him ache with sensation. Bast's cock began to fill again, rising to meet his passion.

"Fuck!" He turned Bast around and kicked his legs apart, finding his lover's opening unerringly.

He pushed inside, moaning as that hot body closed around his cock. Bast pushed back against him, his lover beginning to ride him furiously, the steaming water making them both slick.

Between Bast's body, tight and hot and unbelievably soft flesh around him, and the water sluicing over his back, there was no way he was going to last long. He braced his arms against the tiles on either side of Bast's head, pressing his right forearm against Bast's mouth. "Please, baby-boy."

His answer was a snarl, Bast's teeth sinking deep as the sheer force of desire washed over Trick. He came, a scream pushing from his lungs as his back arched, shoving his hips hard against Bast's buttocks. The pleasure started in his cock and in his forearm, where fangs sank deep, pushing out over him in waves.

He could feel the pull at his arm, Bast's lips fastened tight as they suckled, Bast's ass riding his throbbing cock. His mouth was open wide, he wanted to tell his baby-boy he loved him, loved this, was made for it, but all that came out were incoherent moans and soft whimpers. He leaned forward, wrapping his lips around the skin of Bast's left shoulder blade, imitating his lover's sucking rhythm.

They sank together to the floor, Bast's mouth easing away from his flesh, body still tight and rocking upon his half-hard cock. He reached around and wrapped his hand around Bast's erection, letting his teeth sink into Bast's skin.

"Trick!" That dark head fell back into his shoulder, the full, dark lips open, the stain of blood upon him.

His cock grew hard again at the sight and he pumped weakly; his strength was spent but his body didn't care.

Bast licked his lips, his fangs flashing. "Feels so good. I can feel your heart beating inside me."

He moaned, hand tightening around Bast's hardness as he continued to pump into that tight body. His eyes drifted closed and his breath caught; he couldn't tell where he ended and Bast began, couldn't tell if the blood he felt pumping was moving through his own veins or Bast's.

Bast tightened around him, seed splashing over his hand, hotter than the water. He whimpered as his lover's pleasure became his own, body shuddering, throbbing.

Bast sighed softly, purring low as he sank against the tiles. "Good. So good."

He reached over and turned off the water, his skin too sensitive to bear the flow anymore, and then settled against Bast, arms wrapping around his lover.

"Love you."

"Mm... me, too, Sweets." Bast's hands landed over his. "We really need a mattress in here."

He chuckled and moved, shifting until he was on his back, Bast on top of him. "That should be close enough -- all my bones have melted."

Bast grinned against his chest, nibbling lazily upon his collarbone. "Mm... melted Trick. Delicious."

"Dinner *and* dessert -- I'm honored."

"Oh no, lover... dessert's what happens when I show you what came in the mail today." There was another nip to his nipple, this one sharper and harder. "How do you feel about inflatable, vibrating plugs, Sweets?"

He moaned as his cock twitched, desperate to come back to life. "I'm not going to walk straight for a week." He grinned and pinched Bast's ass. "And neither are you."

Bast grinned at him. "Good thing I don't have any pressing engagements, isn't it?"

"Oh, I think something's pressing all right." He found the energy to roll them over, pushing Bast's hips into the ceramic. "I think it's going to be pressing for a long time."

Lowering his head, he took a hard kiss; just washed Bast was just about the sexiest thing ever. Except for in the shower Bast, or feeding Bast, or Dom Bast, or sub Bast, or...

# Chapter Ten

Porn. Spam. Porn. Spam. Spam. Spam.

Bast sighed. Email was getting less and less interesting -- grow your cock, teens fuck animals, liquidate your debt, nude pics now of eighteenth century political figures... Ooooh... Fetish store liquidating.

He clicked the link, bouncing happily on his belly on the mattress. Cock-rings, nipple clamps, hot wax, vibrators, dildos, plugs, paddles and whips and...

"Hey, Sweets? Do we have vibrating nipple clamps?"

Trick looked up from his game of Civilization. "Don't tell me you're cruising the porn shops on the Internet again. You spent three thousand dollars the last time you did that." Trick laughed. "And yet, no, we still don't have vibrating nipple clamps. And we had to give Rose hers back about a month ago."

"Really? Cool. You want silver or gold? Oh, and they

have a really pretty cock ring -- blood red metal." He stretched out on his belly, searching through the dildos happily.

"Blood red? That would look fantastic wrapped around your cock."

A moment later Trick's weight settled down against his back, his Sweets as naked as he was. A hand came over his shoulder, finger pointing out a rather large crimson dildo. "And that would look amazing going into your ass."

Bast shuddered, the screen going hazy for a second. "You think so? Not the silver one?" His thighs parted, Trick's legs settling between his, weight solid on top of him, making him wriggle.

"Oh, I think the silver one would look amazing going into your ass as well. That thick black one though -- that's for your mouth." Trick hit the page down arrow as he settled more against Bast, the heat of Trick's growing cock finding its home, nestled between Bast's cheeks.

"Now see -- that mask and handcuff set -- the black leather one. I'd like to see you in that. On your knees, legs spread, bent just ever so slightly forward -- the silver dildo up your ass, the black one gagging you. I'm not sure though -- nipple clamps just might be superfluous at that point." Trick nipped at his ear. "Especially vibrating ones."

"Fuck..." He arched back against Trick, eyes focused on the screen, mind filled by the picture Trick was painting. Between Trick's words and Trick's heat, he was hard, just beginning to ache.

"Yeah, baby-boy, that's kind of the idea." Trick's hips began to move, tiny circles that rubbed Trick's cock along Bast's crack. "Maybe I wouldn't use the blindfold. I'd want you to see me fucking my hand and you'd know that I was hard and coming because of how fucking hot you looked."

Oh, fuck -- Bast bit his lip, fists clenching around the laptop. He pushed against Trick's cock, body stretching and hungry. "Sweets. Shit, you make me hot."

Trick's mouth moved down to his neck, nuzzling the skin through his hair, tongue snaking out to draw lewd pictures on his skin. "Place the order, Bast. Pay for the express shipping and we can be doing that tomorrow."

"Oh, yeah." With stuttering fingers, he pushed the buttons and filled out the form, focus on Trick's breath on his nape, his shoulder. Finally the process was finished, and he shut the laptop with a click. "Done."

"Thank fucking God." Trick's knees pushed his legs farther apart, the hard cock pushing into his body in a single long, slow movement.

"Trick! Sweets!" He stretched, riding the sweet burn, letting it sink into his muscles. "Yes."

Trick's hands slid to his arms, wrapping around his biceps, holding him tight. The warm lips found his skin, just above his spine and closed around it, sucking strongly. Then Trick began to fuck him.

Bast's head spun, caught between Trick's lips and cock. The sensations created a line of burning electricity that sent him soaring, gasping. Faster and harder, both mouth and prick moved against him, into him, Trick's body hot and slick and urgent.

His hand slid beneath him, pumping his cock in time with the strokes. Hot, he was fucking hot, Trick's cock slamming into him, sparkles appearing behind his eyes. Trick's mouth left his skin long enough for his Sweets to mutter something about love or fucking or blood or life or come and then Trick's teeth began to worry Bast's skin, biting and pulling.

Bast cried out, body convulsing hard upon Trick's cock, the sweet mixture of pleasure and pain sending him soaring.

"Fuck!" Trick's shout came hot on the heels of his own climax, liquid heat filling him. Trick kept moving, thrusts slowing until they were little more than the same small circular movements of Trick's hips.

"Oh... wow." Bast turned his head, nibbling at Trick's wrist. "So good, Sweets."

"You're so fucking hot." Trick shuddered and his cock shifted inside Bast, sliding along his prostate.

Bast groaned, body rippling with bright shocks. "Fuck, Sweets. Nothing feels like you, fucking me, taking me."

"Feeding you." Trick pressed his wrist against Bast's mouth, hard enough to rub skin against teeth.

"Yes." He nipped gently, just breaking the skin, letting slow drops of blood slid over his tongue.

A long shudder went through Trick, his cock pulsing and growing completely hard again inside Bast's body. "More."

"More?" He bit again, not enough to send Trick flying, but enough to send pleasure and need rocketing through his Sweets.

Another shudder, moving like a ripple through the warm body atop and inside his own. "Y-yes."

He licked at the drops that flowed for him, drinking Trick in.

"More, baby-boy, please. Feed." Trick's voice was thick, dark with need.

"Trick. Need you." He growled, biting deep, pulling

strongly at the wrist, sobbing as Trick's life poured through him.

Trick's scream vibrated against his spine, more seed splashing hotly into him. Trick continued to shudder, soft sobbing noises pressed against Bast's skin. He hummed against the wet flesh, drinking deep, loath to let their connection fade. Finally the hunger eased and he let his tongue close the wound, licking and tasting lazily.

Trick was a familiar, heavy weight against his back, soft breaths sliding through his hair. "Mm... so good," murmured Trick.

"Yes, Sweets. Love you." He kissed the pink line on Trick's wrist, tenderness and bliss filling him.

A sharp, playful nip sparked brightly on his shoulder. "Love you, too, Bast."

"Mmm... good." He floated, eyes closed for a long minute, then something occurred to him and he cursed loudly.

At Trick's questioning noise, he muttered, "I *still* didn't get the vibrating clamps."

Trick laughed. "Seems to me like your memory's going. You getting old, baby-boy?"

"Fucking ancient, Sweets. Fucking *ancient*." He grinned, nuzzling against Trick's arm.

Trick wormed one hand beneath Bast's belly, sliding down to wrap around his cock, pulling it to life. "You're only as old as you feel -- and you don't feel so old to me."

"Oh..." Bast pushed into Trick's hand. "We going for a record, Sweets?"

"I'm not sure I'm up to matching our original thirty-eight times, but I'm willing to make a real effort to hitting thirty-two."

"Like the way you think." He turned, wriggling to face his lover with a smile. "Kiss me."

"I thought you'd never ask." His lips were covered, Trick's tongue pressing past them, pushing deep and hard. Bast curled his arms and legs around those lean hips, holding tight.

"You're like a leech," Trick said, chuckling and licking a trail along Bast's collarbone. "You hang tight and suck out my blood."

He laughed, Trick's tongue and words tickling him equally. "Yeah, but I'm your leech and you wouldn't know what to do without me."

"Explode from excess blood."

"We couldn't possibly have that. Think of the mess."

"It would look like someone had a vampire food-fight."

Bast leaned back and looked at him, laughing aloud. "A vampire food-fight?"

"Yeah, you know -- blood everywhere."

He chuckled, warm through to his toes. He reached up and tangled his fingers in Trick's hair, pulling their faces together. "You are a sick, sick man, Sweets. How I adore you."

Trick laughed, rubbing their noses together. Then his mouth was on Bast's again, kissing him like Trick was going to devour him.

Bast moaned, pressing up into Trick's solid heat. So hungry -- Trick's need was smooth whiskey and dark chocolate pleasure, sliding through him, filling him deep within where the blood couldn't even reach.

Trick was hard again, cock like a brand against Bast's skin. "So hot -- don't ever want to stop fucking you."

"Never. Want to feel you forever, Sweets." His words

were thick, passion and pleasure flavored with desire. Nothing felt like Trick, in his arms, in his body, beneath his tongue -- nothing ever had. "Forever."

Trick kissed him for a long time, body heavy and right on top of him, tongue deep -- demanding, begging, loving. Hours or minutes later, maybe it was even only seconds, it didn't matter, Trick's mouth left his to explore his skin. Trick sucked on his chin and licked along his neck, tongue spending long moments in the hollow of his throat.

He stretched out, belly and cock sliding against Trick's skin, making them both shiver. "You make me feel so good, Sweets."

"Good." Trick's voice was muffled against his skin.

Trick kept tasting him: teeth scraping across his collarbone and lips closing over his shoulder, sucking and licking until Trick moved on to bite at the muscle of his arm and tease the crease of his elbow with a wicked tongue.

Melting. He was melting and flying and purring and completely bewitched, entranced by his Sweets' tongue and lips. He shifted on the bed, incoherently moaning, all good sense thrown out in favor of experiencing this perfect pleasure.

Trick continued his explorations down to Bast's hand. Each finger was sucked into the hot mouth, teeth and tongue licking and scraping and nipping at his fingertips before letting go. One after another until index to pinky and thumb had been loved. Then Trick started on his palm. He'd never really thought about how many nerves were in your palm, about how good you could be made to feel, just by someone scraping their teeth along your lifeline.

His free hand slid down to circle his cock, pumping slowly, ratcheting the pleasure that moved up his arm, through his chest, even higher.

Trick moved back up his arm, leaving licks and bites along the way. When he reached Bast's shoulder again he began to lick his way down to Bast's nipple. But Trick didn't lick his nipple, or bite it or suck it or do anything at all to it; instead his Sweets teased the skin around it, drawing close time and again but never touching it.

Trick even pulled the flesh next to it into his mouth and sucked in time with the long, lazy strokes of Bast's hand over his own cock.

"T...tease." The word was gasped, almost sobbed, hips and shoulders twisting to find the right combination of sensation to bring him over the edge.

Trick's mouth left him, his Sweets leaning over him to smile down into his face. "Uh-huh." Trick licked his own lips, slowly, eyes half-closed. "You taste good, baby-boy."

"Oh, fuck, Sweets..." His legs parted farther, hips pumping his cock into his hands. "You make me crazy, so fucking hot, Trick."

Trick's legs were between his, pushing them even farther apart and Trick's hands were on his, pulling him away from his cock. "That's mine." Then Trick's mouth closed over him, just the head of his cock, sucking gently, tongue sliding across his slit.

He writhed, begging softly for more, harder, for Trick to stop the delicious, agonizing, so fucking sweet tease and make him come. Trick let his hands go in favor of cupping his buttocks, tilting him and pushing his cock in and out of Trick's mouth.

Sobbing, he pushed into Trick's throat, screaming his

need and pleasure as he shattered, entire body pulsating.

When he came back to himself, Trick was lying with his head on Bast's hip, licking at his softening cock, looking like the a cat licking cream from his whiskers.

Bast reached down, stroking Trick's hair with a still trembling hand. "Melted my brain."

Trick chuckled. "I don't think that's all that melted."

"Mmm... no. You melted all sorts of important things." He smiled down, running one finger down Trick's nose. "I love you."

Trick kissed his finger. "Oh, good. I love you, too."

He traced the full, kiss-swollen lips, letting his joy and admiration and simple love shine through.

Tricks eyes were bright and shinning, his hands moving randomly over Bast's skin as he nuzzled into Bast's touches.

He moved down so he could taste Trick's mouth, the kiss lazy and slow, motions familiar and easy as breathing.

"I love the way you taste. Your mouth, your skin, your cock, your come. It all tastes like you but it's all different, too." Trick pressed close to him, hands roaming over his back and along his ass, the touches bringing pleasure and claiming possession.

"Mm... feels good." He bent his head, nibbling gently on Trick's neck, tasting and laving the oft-sampled flesh.

Bast felt Trick's cock jerk against him, his Sweets tilting his head back. The movements were automatic, ingrained; he was pretty sure Trick didn't even realize he was doing it anymore.

"Just fed, love. Don't need to bite. I just wanted to taste you, that's all." He continued nipping and licking, happy and sated and surrounded by his Sweets.

Trick's legs tangled with his, the warm hands drawing him closer as his lover settled.

Completely happy, so happy it felt obscene and luxurious, Bast sucked a series of hickeys on Trick's neck, a long line of tiny marks patterning the smooth skin. Trick was making soft noises of pleasure, soft and warm against him.

A soft laughed moved his hair. "What would Rose and Bael think now, if they saw this? They'd wonder where their kinky vampire had gone."

"He's still here, just letting the much more rare and elusive Sebastian enjoy his lover for a while."

Trick ducked his head and brought their mouths together for a gentle kiss, lips pressing together lightly, tongues playing softly. "I love you, Sebastian Apostolos, all of you."

"I know; you're my heartbeat." He stretched along Trick's body, languid and relaxed. "And besides, we have kink planned for tomorrow, at your very seductive request."

"I can't wait to see you all trussed up. Fuck, I'm getting all worked up again just thinking about it." Trick shifted against him, cock warm and hard as it rubbed across his skin.

"Are you sure you want my mouth full? I couldn't do this..." Bast groaned, mouth finding Trick's neck, fangs pressing against, but not piercing, the skin.

Moaning, Trick pressed closer, hips beginning to move rhythmically. "That's cheating," he whispered against Bast's ear.

"Cheating? Would I do that?" He dragged his teeth slowly over the skin, pulling.

"Fuck yes." Trick gasped, starting to hump against

him, hands cupping his ass, pulling him against each thrust.

He chuckled. "Only every fucking chance I get, Sweets."

Then he bit down, piercing Trick's skin and letting the dark richness of blood fill his mouth. Trick screamed, pulling him tight against the pulsing cock as seed splashed between them, hot and fragrant.

He didn't drink long, just enough to sate and enjoy and relish, tongue cleaning the blood from Trick thoroughly.

"Oh, I definitely think you're going to be gagged by that cock. Otherwise you'll just keep cheating." Trick gave him a lazy, sloppy, wet kiss. "And I want to come all over you first."

Bast shivered. "And saying things like that isn't cheating?"

Trick chuckled. "And then I'll take that big, cold cock out of your mouth and put mine in -- you can suck me and feed from me while you come."

"You bastard. It's going to take *forever* for tomorrow to get here."

Trick's chuckles turned to laughter. "You could always while away the time ordering more toys on the Internet. After all, you still don't have vibrating nipple clamps."

Trick grabbed his wrists suddenly holding his hands above his head. "Or we could get warmed up for the big event."

He flexed his muscles, rolling them over easily, covering Trick's body with his own. "Sounds like a plan, Sweets. You're it first."

# Chapter Eleven

Trick took the beer from the bartender and took a long swallow, looking around the room with narrowed eyes. A BDSM club. He still wasn't sure how he'd let Bast talk him into coming; he didn't like fucking in public -- private parties were one thing, this was quite another. But there had been something in his lover's eyes when he'd spoken about showing Trick off, showing the world *his* boy.

Trick had known at that moment that he wanted to do it, wanted to give Bast the pleasure of taking him in public, of letting the world see that Bast *owned* him. It was the truth, after all.

He refused to wear a leash and collar. Refused to wear anything other than his usual basic black jeans and black t-shirt, black leather jacket thrown over top.

Bast had laughed and muttered something about how

a proper sub would do as he was told. Trick had just grinned and pressed close and murmured, "But where would be the challenge in that?"

He'd agreed to come on his own, to meet Bast at the club. It gave him a chance to be early and check the place out. The place wasn't packed, but there were quite a few people there. A number of them were wearing collars and leashes and one poor guy was crawling on his hands and knees. A few were dancing, most were mingling, greeting friends and chatting or checking out the equipment on the raised dais in the center of the room.

Trick chewed on the inside of his lips, nervous anticipation making him hard, making him feel stretched and tight, even the soft material of his t-shirt scratching.

He'd been here almost a half hour now, nursing his beer and his "I'm taken" vibes at the bar.

There was no sign of Bast.

A rather large woman, black and white hair slicked back and body encased in dark rubber, came to stand beside him, ordering a glass of wine. Her eyes ranged over Trick lazily and then she met his gaze. "You're a fine piece of work. You available to play?"

Before he could answer, a cool, familiar hand fell on his neck, fingers rubbing lightly over the vein. "No, he's not. Not tonight anyway. Tonight I want him for myself."

Trick turned toward his lover, eyes widening as he took in the sight. Dressed in a surprisingly simple black turtleneck and slacks, Bast looked elegant, quiet -- classy as hell.

"You look great, like a slice of night." He wanted to move into Bast's arms and kiss him, but he wasn't sure about the protocol and he hesitated.

Bast beamed at him and held out a pale hand, body moving closer. "Thanks, Sweets. Kiss me."

He didn't need to be told twice. Moving into Bast's arms he slid his arms around the trim waist, mouth opening as it met his lover's. His lover tasted like really old scotch and lingering woodsmoke and something that just meant Bast, something that reminded him of citrus fruit and blood and really good sex.

One hand tangled up in his hair, Bast kissing him long and slow, purring softly against his lips. When their mouths parted, Bast's mouth moved to his ear. "Let's go find us a nice divan to curl up on, watch the show. You make me hungry, Sweets."

"I thought we were the show?"

"Maybe later." He felt Bast's smile. "The stage is a bit public for vamping out and I'm not sure I could stop myself from nibbling. Besides, the stage is mainly for the paying curious. The real fun happens in the dark corners."

"I don't know," he said, bumping Bast's hip with his own. "I'd say the real fun happens wherever you are." He took another kiss and then linked his fingers with Bast's. "Where you go, I will follow."

"Mm... my sweet boy." Bast trailed his fingers through Trick's hair. "Of course, I do want a seat beneath the lights, where people can admire my Sweets and be incredibly envious of me. After all, I have the best looking partner here."

Bast led him through the room, taking a very obvious and winding path to a long dark couch on the most outer edge of the circle of lights focused on the stage.

Trick sprawled out on the couch and looked up. His lover's eyes glittered down at him. "You get off on it, don't you -- on showing me off?"

"Yes. I love the way you look, the way you walk." Bast settled beside Trick, trailing a finger down his midsection. "And I love knowing you trust me, that you love me. That they might look, might even touch, but this..." He tapped the area above Trick's left nipple. "This is mine."

"For always." His voice was a little husky and he had to clear his throat, but much as he tried, he couldn't find anything flippant to say. Instead he covered Bast's hand with his own.

"For always." Bast leaned forward, taking a long, hard kiss, body plastered against him. The noise, the people, the club faded back as his lover filled his senses.

He wrapped his arms around that sweet body, hands sliding into the sedately black hair. His body rose to the call of Bast's, hips pushing his erection into his lover's belly.

Bast's hand slid beneath his hip, pulling him closer, their bodies beginning to rock together instinctively. Bast was hard against his thigh, mouth hungry and eager.

"Fuck -- you're the only person I know who can make me come in my pants."

"Everybody's gotta have a talent, Sweets." Bast bent his head and nuzzled at Trick's throat. "I'm not being very dom-y am I? I just get so distracted by how good you smell, how you taste -- I forget to play and just need you."

"Need you, too." Trick bent his head back further, giving Bast more neck to play at. "Need you so bad, baby-boy."

"Oh, fuck, Sweets." He felt Bast's shudder, felt the hand on his hip tighten. Little soft licks and nips and kisses covered his throat and jaw, sharp teeth just threatening every few moments.

He felt each scrape of teeth like a wave that ended at the base of his spine and in his balls, making him harder and hotter and he whimpered very softly. "Are you going to tease me like this all night?"

"Mmm... probably, yes." Bast's voice was distracted, lips worrying the tender spot where the vampire bit most often. Trick shuddered; Bast loved to suck there for what seemed like hours, curling in close, hands petting slowly, keeping him lost in pleasure.

Trick's hands slid slowly down over Bast's back, not stopping until he had that tight ass in his hands, pulling his lover down as he ground up into familiar heat. Bast hummed against his skin, the sound vibrating through him. Bast's body rocked down against him, rhythmic and sensual.

He was making noises, probably embarrassing noises, but he couldn't stop himself, didn't want to stop; he just wanted Bast to keep on doing what he was doing. And to feed. He always wanted Bast to feed, to take blood from him and keep himself alive... or animated or whatever it was he called it, which really, didn't matter just now.

"You make me so hungry." This admission was followed by another nip, this one sharper, full of intent.

He arched his head back even farther, begging silently. "Please..." Well, almost silently.

Bast lifted his head, eyes glittering. "No screaming. Don't scare the mortals. You scream, I'll stop. Deal?"

"Fuck. I'll try." He didn't think it was possible, not with how good Bast made him feel, but maybe if he bit his lip or his fingers or his hand or his whole arm he'd be able to keep from screaming.

"Unless you want me to stop. Find a back room."

Bast leaned down, licking Trick's ear. "Let me bite your cock..."

A shudder worked its way through him. "Fuck yes!"

It was all he could do not to push Bast down to his groin to start right now.

Bast stood, stance slightly shaky, running his fingers through his hair. The room was filling, naked flesh lit up upon the stage. Soft murmurs and chuckles and moans colored the air. Bast held out his hand to Trick, eyes hot and glowing with hunger. "Come on, Sweets."

He grabbed that hand, letting the vampire pull him up. "Let's hurry."

This time the path to the bar was nowhere near as winding, Bast exchanging cash for key and then leading Trick behind the stage where they were shown to a well-appointed room filled with a bed almost as big as theirs.

The door shut and locked behind them. "Sweets."

"Fuck, Bast." He leaned against the back of the door and his hands pushed at Bast's shoulders. "Do it, baby-boy."

Bast didn't argue, didn't tease, just sank to his knees, hands fumbling with Trick's jeans. Once the buttons popped free, the hot, hungry mouth engulfed him.

He grabbed onto Bast's shoulders, body tense, almost shaking; he knew what was coming, wanted it, craved it. He pumped his hips, sliding his cock in and out of the welcoming heat of Bast's mouth. "Please... do it."

Lean hands pressed Trick's hips against the door, Bast's bright eyes shining up at him before the bottom fell out of the universe and Trick drowned in pure pleasure. It made him scream, made him push his hips deep into Bast's mouth, made him come, made him scream some more before the sounds faded into soft whimpers that matched the sweet shudders that flooded his body.

Bast sucked him gently, humming softly, color high. Each long pull made him warm and shivery, made the series of aftershocks feel strong and overwhelming. The only thing holding him up was the door behind him and his own hands on Bast's shoulders and when his lover let his cock slip from between red lips, Trick slid down the door until they were face to face.

"I love you," he whispered.

"Even if I bring you to play dom with and then get so hungry for you I can't wait? Even if this thing we have is really fucking overwhelming and so much more than playing around?" Bast took his lips in a long, breathless kiss. "I love you, Sweets, with all I am."

"Maybe because of that." He shrugged and looped his arms around Bast's neck. "I don't need to fucking analyze it, baby-boy. It just is and nothing's ever felt like it, so I'm holding on and not letting go."

"I love the way you think." Bast stole another kiss. "Bed or back out into the club?"

Trick grinned and licked the corner of Bast's mouth, imagining he could taste his own blood there. "You're the dom," he said with a chuckle.

"Oh, right." Bast laughed, dark eyes shining at him. "I forgot."

"As long as you don't forget where you eat," Trick told Bast, pushing him down onto his back and closing their mouths together. Bast was still hard, pressing up against him restlessly, tongue thrusting into his mouth. His body responded predictably and he pushed Bast into the floor, moaning softly. "If you want to go back out there you'd better say so now."

"Out where?" Bast's hands slid beneath his t-shirt,

pulling it up.

Trick raised himself long enough to help get his t-shirt off and then he covered Bast again, kissing and biting at the red lips. He kicked off his jeans, moaning as they got caught around his ankles. Bast was whimpering against his lips, hands moving restlessly over his body.

"Too many clothes, baby-boy," Trick muttered as he rubbed against Bast.

"Yeah." The affirmative was muffled as Bast yanked the soft black turtleneck up over his head.

Deprived of Bast's lips, Trick went for one of those nipples instead, humming happily as the flesh peaked, as if reaching up for his touch. He fumbled at Bast's pants, not really trying to attempt the button one-handed, just enjoying the heat and hardness of Bast's cock against his hand through the material.

"Oh, fuck! 's good..." Bast writhed, throwing the turtleneck aside, hips pushing up against Trick's touch.

Long, trembling fingers worked the button loose and a wiggle and a thrust later, Trick had his arms full of naked, hard vampire.

Trick moaned as he rubbed against silky flesh. "What do you want, baby-boy? Anything you want -- you know it's yours."

"You. Need you. Fuck, I'm aching for you." Bast's legs wrapped around his waist, body rocking against him.

Trick flipped over to his back, pulling Bast with him, letting the vampire drive their coupling. He slid one hand between them, pinching and tugging at Bast's nipple.

Bast moaned, arching and shuddering as they rocked together. "Yes. Yes, please. More."

"Want you to fuck me," he whispered as his other

hand found Bast's other nipple and began to play.

"Yes. Oh, shit. Yes." Bast shuddered and then pulled away, standing with a low cry. "Bed, Sweets. Now, or I'll come before I'm inside you."

He crawled over to the bed, getting up onto all fours on it and looking over his shoulder, groaning at the sight of Bast, utterly naked, cock red and hard. "Like this?"

Bast shuddered, moving up behind him. Bast's hands rubbed his ass and a soft kiss was brushed against the small of his back. "Yes. Just like that."

Then that rough tongue, hot and slick, pressed against his entrance. He wailed, all thoughts fleeing as he pressed back into the slick touch. Bast licked him relentlessly, fucking him with that talented, hungry tongue, hands sliding over his thighs and back.

"Fuck, Bast. Gonna come," he warned, rocking back into each thrust of Bast's tongue.

The heat disappeared, Bast's fingers circling the base of his cock. "Wait for me, Sweets. Hold on." Then Bast's skin covered his back, hard cock pressing inside him.

"Oh, fuck, yes." He pushed back, urging his lover to fill him. "Hard and fast, baby-boy, I want to feel you."

"Yes." Bast thrust hard, hands strong on his hips, pulling him into each motion. "So fucking hot. So good."

He sobbed, spreading his knees further, head dropping onto his hand as he pushed back, eagerly meeting each of Bast's thrusts. Bast rode him hard, sweet cries pouring down around him, letting Trick know he was not alone in his hunger, in his need. Higher and higher Bast pushed him until he could feel the explosion coming, feel it building in his spine, in his balls, in his toes.

"Close, Trick. Gonna... oh, Sweets!" The jumbled

words were superseded by a low cry as heat filled him.

He wailed again, his own orgasm shooting from him.

Bast pulled them both over, wrapping his arm around Trick. "My Chosen."

He nuzzled into the vampire, sliding his cheek against sweat-slicked skin. "I love you, Bast. So much."

"Mm... I bet I lose my 'I'm a big, macho dom' card." Bast chuckled and nibbled lightly on his skin. "Oh, wait. I'm short and skinny and let Rose beat my ass... that's probably why they didn't issue me a laminated one to begin with, huh?"

Trick laughed and licked sweet-salt from Bast's skin. "You can top me anytime, baby-boy."

"You're so good to me, Sweets." Bast grinned. "Does that mean you'll wear the leash and collar?"

"Yes. But not in public, baby-boy. Not in public."

"Mm... it's a deal, slaveboy." Bast stretched and kissed him soundly. "Can I be the harem boy tomorrow?"

"No, wait, I've got a good one. You can be the big bad vampire and I'll be the helpless rentboy under your thrall."

"Ooooooh! That sounds like fun... Wait!" Bast looked at him, wide-eyed. "I *always* have to be the vampire."

He laughed. "That's because you've got the teeth for it." He leaned in and licked inside Bast's mouth, shivering as his tongue found the sharp incisors and stroked over them.

"Oh, yeah." Bast nipped his lip, licking the blood away easily. "Mmm... how about we play I'm a slinky, desperately in love vampire and you're the sexy, delicious boy who stole my heart?"

He jerked at the nip, hips pushing against Bast

automatically. "I think I can live with that, baby-boy."

Bast chuckled. "Want more, Sweets?" Bast bent his head and nibbled at Trick's neck.

"Fuck yes. Always." His hands found Bast's shoulders, holding on as he anticipated the rush. His head dropped back in a practiced move, exposing the length of his vein to Bast, even as he rubbed his growing erection against Bast's skin.

"Oh. Oh, Sweets."

The rush as Bast's teeth entered his skin was sweet. He came with a sob, body shuddering and shaking as he held onto his lover in a tight, grasping grip. Bast suckled slowly, letting the pleasure pour over Trick in slow waves.

He sobbed with each suck, red sparkling behind his closed lids. Eventually the sensations eased and Trick drifted, held close in Bast's arms. He was warm and sated and happy, curled against Bast.

"My Sweets. Love you so." Hands trailed through his hair, caressing him gently.

"Mmm...me, too," he mumbled against warm skin.

"Sleep, Sweets. We've got the room for as long as we want it."

"Okay..."

He snuggled closer, letting the sweet lassitude pull him down into sleep and dreams of wearing Bast's collar.

# Chapter Twelve

Trick woke up squished between the wall and Bear's bulk. In fact Rose's significant other had his arm flung over Trick's midsection and he was snoring like a fucking jack hammer. He tried to slip out, but Bear just pushed up against him, snuffling once and then going back to cutting through concrete.

So he elbowed the big guy. That got him a grunt and then more snores, but Bear also rolled back far enough that Trick was able to crawl out of the bed.

Scratching his belly, he picked his way through the bodies on the floor, looking for Bast.

The last he'd seen his lover, Rose and some of her pain junkie friends were paddling his ass, Bast eating it up with a fucking spoon. Trick had found the twins and fucked them until he fell asleep. He wasn't sure how he wound up on the bed with Bear and the four others crowded next to the big guy, but it didn't really matter.

He'd been good all fucking evening and late into the night, sharing his vampire with the others, letting them play with their favorite boy -- now it was his turn.

He'd wandered through Rose's apartment twice without finding his lover when he realized the shower was running. And he knew.

That was where he'd find Bast.

Sure enough, the vampire was leaning against the wall of Rose's shower, hot spray hitting him full in the face, on his chest, pounding against the not quite hard cock.

He let the door close quietly behind him and leaned casually against the counter. "Looks like you've got a little something left over for me."

Bast didn't turn toward him, but the smile that crept around the wet face was warm and genuine, cock firming visibly beneath the water. "I was hoping you'd come looking for me, Sweets. I always save the best for last."

"Good."

He pushed the glass door aside and climbed into the shower, getting between Bast and his spray. He waited until Bast's eyes opened and then grinned at his lover. "Show me what you've got, baby-boy."

Bast's smile widened, became almost feral. He leaned back, one hand beginning to slowly pump his cock, the other trailing down his neck, where a half-dozen pink marks were fading. "You like what you see, Sweets?"

He slowly looked that lean body up and down, gaze lingering on the hard cock, and then on the sharp teeth that Bast's smile revealed. "Oh yeah, I think I do."

"Oh, good." Bast's gaze roamed along his body, beginning to glow as they devoured him. "Because you look edible."

"Oh, I was hoping you were hungry." He leaned against Bast, rubbing eagerly against the water-slicked skin. "I was hoping you'd want to suck me off, hoping you'd want to feed, hoping you'd want to fuck."

"Fuck, yes, Trick." Their lips met, Bast's mouth open and hungry, tongue pushing into him eagerly. Bast wrapped around him, both arms and a leg, holding him tight.

He bit at the swollen lips, hungry for Bast's flavor, gasping as it wiped away the taste of all the others he'd fucked.

Bast devoured him, pulling his tongue into the hungry mouth and sucking. The thin body almost crawled up him, fingers tangled in his hair, moaning low. He shoved Bast hard against the tiles, driving their cocks together, fingers crawling over Bast's skin.

Bast's mouth left his, lips finding his ear. "No matter how many times I come, I'm not done, not satisfied until I have you inside me, Sweets."

Moaning, he pushed Bast higher against the wall, hands finding the delicious ass, spreading his lover's cheeks, tilting that amazing body. "You want me, baby-boy?"

"Fuck, yes. Need you, Trick." Bast's head fell to his shoulder, lips finding his throat, teeth nipping his skin.

A shudder ran through him at the touch and he shoved himself into Bast's body, the tight passage still slick from countless fucks.

Bast's groan was loud, delicious, sharp as fangs against his throat. "Yes. Yes, Trick."

He slammed into his lover's body, over and over. He wanted so badly, he could hear his own blood in his veins. "Bast."

"Hungry for you. Need you, Sweets. I'm hungry." Bast babbled against his skin, body hunching against him, moving into each thrust.

"Yes, baby-boy, yes. I need it, too. Want it. I want it."

He was thrusting blindly now, pushing into Bast's body with little grace, driven by need and lust and love and want. Bast struck quickly, the muscles around his cock convulsing as the sharp teeth slid deep, pulling pleasure out of every nerve, drowning him in sensation.

He threw his head back, screaming, coming, spilling himself into Bast, hot come, hot blood, hot life flowing between them. Bast fed, pulling and suckling long after the echoes of his screams had faded. The touches of his baby-boy's tongue were soothing, hot and soft and sweet all at once. Shudders moved through him until at last they disappeared, leaving him leaning heavily against Bast, pushing Bast into the wall.

"Love you, Sweets. " Bast nuzzled and nipped, lips hot against his throat.

"Fuck, I love you, Bast." He shivered and laughed and let Bast slide slowly down. "So fucking much."

"Mmm... so good." Bast shared a kiss with him, then moved into the cooling water. "Do we have time to get home, Sweets? Before the sun rises?"

"Yeah, the clock in the kitchen said 4:06 -- we should be able to make it if we hurry."

"I'll call a cab. I want to sleep in our own bed." Bast grinned up, eyes twinkling mischievously. "I'm too old for this six in a bed shit."

Trick laughed and grabbed Bast, kissing him hard. He would have taken Bast up against the wall again except that he was truly exhausted now and he wanted to be home almost as badly as his lover did.

Orgies could be fun, but at the start of the day, there was nowhere like home.

# Chapter Thirteen

Trick threw himself down on the divan, lying sprawled out, hand tapping against the arm arhythmically. He got up again a moment later, striding into the kitchen and going into the fridge.

He stared into it for a few minutes, though he knew its contents by heart. Citrus fruit, steaks and blood. He was half way tempted to grab the blood and heat it up, eat it. Just to see what Bast would do. The truth was that he was bored and restless and Bast had been distracted and moody.

He wandered back toward their bed, where Bast was reading, and tickled his lover's feet.

"Hey, Sweets. Whatcha need?" Bast's eyes flicked up from his book, but his chin didn't lift.

He shrugged and sat down hard on the bed, bouncing. He tickled Bast's feet again. Bast made a low rumbling noise and inched his feet away, turning the page. Frowning, Trick slid his hand along Bast's inner thigh and then pinched his lover's skin.

"Damn it!" Bast slammed the book shut and lifted his head, eyes flashing. "What?"

He shrugged again, two fingers walking along Bast's thigh. "Nothing."

"Trick..." Bast glared for a minute, legs shifting. "You pinched me. You must want *something*."

"I didn't pinch you -- I gave you a love tug." He walked his fingers up to the edge of Bast's hip and pinched the skin there between his fingers. "That's a pinch."

"You son of a bitch!" Bast scooted over to the head of the bed, rubbing his hip. "Have I pissed you off or something?"

He flung himself along the bed and let his foot tap against Bast's. "'m not pissed off."

"No? You want to go out maybe?" Bast's book bounced and fell beside the bed and Bast leaned over to grab it.

Trick watched himself lean forward and goose Bast. Laughter spilled from him at his lover's yelp and he lay in the bed, giggling up at the ceiling.

It took Bast a second to grab the book, the thin hand pushing it on the mattress a moment before the warning growl sounded. Then, with the speed that was so easy to forget about, Bast was straddling his chest, his wrists held in one preternaturally strong hand, a hank of rope held in the other.

"No. I don't think we're going out this evening. I think we should stay in." With those growled words, Bast bound his wrists firmly, lashing them to the hook in the headboard.

A shiver went through him. Anticipation and need, it settled in the base of his spine, flaring out from there, red hot and delicious. He shifted his hips. "Well, aren't you just the big tough vampire?"

"Don't make me gag you, Sweets." Bast stood up, moved off the bed. "You don't like it and I want to be able to kiss you."

He opened his mouth on another sassy comment, biting his lip at the last minute as he tested the tightness of the ropes that bound his wrists. They were pretty tight. Bast watched him for a second, then nodded, trailing one hand down his thigh before heading to the closet where they kept their toys.

Anticipation cut away the boredom and restlessness like a knife moving through butter as he watched Bast's slender body move easily, the muscles shifting beneath sleek skin. He licked his lips.

His baby-boy walked back and forth, hands full of silk rope one time, a steel bar beneath his arm the next. Bottles and chains and a black plug and a tiny curved knife were all arranged neatly at the end of the bed. All the while Bast hummed quietly, face peaceful. Finally he shut the closet and wandered over to start some music, low and dark. He extinguished the lights, locked up the elevator and turned off the phone.

Tension coiled through Trick's muscles, bubbled through his veins with his blood and settled like electricity in his bones. He wanted to ask what Bast was planning; it was on the tip of his tongue and he almost spoke more than once. Each time that part of him that was convinced that not knowing would be more exciting won out.

But he was nearly vibrating in place by the time Bast returned to the bed.

Bast reached out and stroked his cheek. “You want a blindfold, Sweets?”

No, he was pretty sure he didn’t. Not with all the stuff Bast had brought out, half of it he didn’t even recognize or know what it was for. He wet his lips. “If you want me to.”

“Mmm...” Bast leaned forward and kissed him hard and deep, tongue and teeth devouring him, making him dizzy, the motion at odds with the earlier stillness. Then Bast backed away, leaving him gasping.

Suddenly Bast was at the foot of the bed, fingers circling one of his ankles, lifting it to the open mouth. Sharp fangs scraped upon his skin, just threatening, before a wide leather cuff was fastened on. His other leg received the same treatment -- a long caress, a teasing nibble, and then it was encased in leather.

He moaned softly. His cock was hard, his nipples peaked and reaching and, so far, Bast had barely touched him. The anticipation was going to kill him.

Insistent hands hooked his ankles to either end of the metal bar, assuring that his legs stayed spread and open.

Warm hands slid up his thighs, moving to cup his balls, squeezing gently and rhythmically. He took long, deep breaths, trying to quell the tremors that shot through him.

“You were so hungry for attention, Sweets.” Bast began to wrap his balls in thin silk rope as he spoke, the material holding him tight. “Poking and pushing and restless. Did you not think I saw you? I can smell your moods, the heat of your blood just under your skin.”

Once his balls were wrapped, Bast started on his cock, pulling the silk tight and even.

Helpless, bound and held in place, the entire focus

of his lover. It was exactly what he'd needed, what he'd been restlessly searching for. Bast could do anything he wanted, would do anything he wanted and Trick could only lie there and enjoy it. Wearing Bast's restraints, he found the freedom to submit to his lover's will. A shiver of delight danced along his spine.

Bast continued wrapping him, hands cool on his throbbing flesh. "You're so hot, you make me hungry. Should I take a taste of you, drink you in?"

The ribbons were fastened off below the head of his cock, making it seem huge, dark against the white cloth. Bast leaned down, sucked the exposed flesh into his mouth and pulled, tugging with lips and tongue. Trick screamed as pleasure shot from his cock out over his nerves. He arched his back, shoving himself up as far as possible.

The heat and pressure peaked and then disappeared, Bast backing away to suck at his inner thigh. "So hungry, Sweets."

Trick was, he was so hungry. He could feel each throb of his blood through his veins, highlighted by the way it felt in his cock: thick and vital, and in his wrists and his ankles. Bast sucked against the tender skin of his thighs, little nips here and there sending electric shocks through him. Suddenly slick fingers slid into his cleft, pressing insistently against his entrance.

"Let me in, Sweets. Want to touch you deep." The words were accompanied by the flick of a tongue against his silk-wrapped sacs.

He shuddered, a moan passing his lips as he bore down on Bast's fingers.

Bast's soft moan answered his, fingers sliding deep, pressing and pushing. His lover didn't tease, finger-fucked him with hard, steady strokes that sent him higher and higher and keep him there. The maddening bites moved over his hips and belly.

His breath was coming in hard, short gasps, and he was whimpering, little noises that he couldn't have stopped even if he had wanted to. Bound as he was, he couldn't control any of it, couldn't really even move into the sensations; he was forced to simply experience them.

"So lovely, my needy one." Teeth scraped against his ribs, fingers curling against his gland. "I want to sink my teeth into you, drink you in until we're lost -- all fucking and blood and love."

He shouted out, body jerking, arching, shaking. If his cock and balls hadn't been bound he would have been coming.

Without warning, Bast was between his bound legs, lifting his hips, thumbs spreading him as the hard cock drew a line of fire inside him. "Look at me, Sweets. Want you to see how hungry you make me."

Bast's face was fierce; he could see himself reflected in the vampire's pupils. He could see his own want and need and hunger reflected there, multiplied exponentially. Every nerve was aflame with harsh, sharp hunger and Bast knew, took it, made it his own.

Bast's hands slid up his arms, holding on as they moved together with hard thrusts, the lean body slamming into him, dark hair falling all around him, tickling his skin. Sharp, biting kisses captured his lips, those dark eyes hot on his face, watching him. Every time Bast slammed into him he made a noise, a sob of need and hunger and fulfillment. Each one was a plea for more, a plea for it to never end, a plea for Bast to take him to that place they could only get to together.

Bast whispered against his lips, needy, husky words

that filled his mind as that long cock filled his body. "Mine. So hot, so tight. My sweet love. My life. I love you. Always see you, Trick. Always need you. You're mine. My Chosen." The words sank into his skin, into his muscles and his bones, adding to the pressure in his cock, his balls.

Bast's motions became harder, faster, the words against his lips become low growls as his lover neared orgasm. He was going to explode. It didn't matter that he was bound; the pleasure was peaking and flowing through him in waves. Every time Bast's cock hit his gland he screamed as the pleasure exploded again inside him; there was no other path for it to leave his body.

"Yes, so good. Yes." Bast stiffened, body going still as heat filled Trick's body.

He sobbed, body twisting in its bindings.

He lay beneath Bast, shuddering and trembling, trying to find his breath, desperate to come.

Bast's hands stroked over him, soft and slick. "Breathe, love. We're not done playing. You can go farther with me; I know it." A soft, slow, deep kiss was given to him, taken from him.

He moaned, another shudder rocking him, and then he concentrated on the kiss, on the way Bast's tongue invaded his mouth, wet and agile. The kisses continued until the urgency lessened, Bast's cock snugged deep within him. Finally those lips left his, black eyes calm and warm. "Going to put the plug in you. Keep you filled and hot so I can touch you, make you fly."

Trick whimpered, another soft tremor going through him. Bast leaned back, rubbing the dark plug between his hands, warming and slicking it. With a gentle motion, Bast pulled out, the plug spreading him with his next breath. He wriggled his hips, gasping at the sensation as the plug moved with him, brushing over his prostate. He stilled, eyes hot on his lover.

"Lovely. You make me hungry." Bast's eyes glowed, fangs bared and sharp.

He whimpered, body jerking. He was gasping again, body trembling with excitement, anticipation. His tongue rubbed over his own teeth, wet his lips and he let his head drop back, offering his neck, hoping to entice his lover.

A pained snarl rent the air, Bast literally pouncing against his chest. Lips touched his throat, not biting, just tasting, low hungry growls filling the air. Sobbing, he pushed his neck against Bast's lips. Each of Bast's growls vibrated against him, shivered down his spine and set his blood thrumming.

"Tempting me. Bad Sweets. Want you. Hungry."

"Need you so bad, baby-boy," he whispered, a soft shudder shaking his body, giving proof to his words.

Bast's tongue slid over his neck, resting heavily on the vein. "My life."

He could feel his own heartbeat, pulsing beneath Bast's tongue. Everything else blurred until all he was flowed through his veins. He could feel the slow slide of Bast's fangs into his skin, feel the pull of blood and the crash of pleasure. He screamed, the sound growing faint beneath the sound of the rush of his blood. He was jerking in his bonds, climaxing, whether or not he actually came. He didn't know, he didn't care, all he knew was pleasure and Bast's mouth, Bast's heartbeat as it matched his own.

Bast's tongue and hands brought him back, the tiny knife slicing away the silk, restraints disappearing as warm hands moved over his skin. "Need you, Trick. Need you so."

He lay still, boneless and relaxed, sated, while Bast cared for him. He could feel Bast's love in every beat of his heart. "Mmm."

"Rest. I've got you. Always." Soft kisses landed on his eyes, his cheeks.

He turned into the kisses, nuzzling, almost purring.

"Sweet love." Bast was wrapped around him, touching him everywhere, keeping him afloat. "So beautiful, so strong. How I love you."

"Feel good," he murmured, nuzzling.

"You do. You didn't have to push, love. I would have given you what you needed."

He shrugged, murmuring happily at the feeling of Bast's skin dragging against him. "I didn't know."

"Mmm... then it's good that I did." Bast nibbled at his collarbone, teeth just grazing. "So sweet."

A soft shudder moved through him. "I love you, babyboy."

"I know, Trick. You're my heartbeat." A soft, heavy blanket covered them both, Bast curling around him, cheek on his shoulder, one hand cupped over his balls, the other resting against his cheek.

He turned his head, licking gently at the fingers, pulling the taste into him, and then nuzzled against Bast's hair. He sighed deeply, happily and let his eyes drift closed. He was safe, loved, melted.

When he woke, Bast was still draped around him, holding him close, dark eyes focused and warm.

# Chapter Fourteen

He was floating. Mid-air and spinning slowly, colors and sounds passing by him and through him. It felt good and right and the only thing missing was Bast.

Trick was trying to fix that but first the key wouldn't go into the call box for the elevator and now he couldn't figure out which button to press.

Someone had changed them, relabeled them or something. It was very frustrating and it was ruining the floaty feeling, making the colors and sounds swirl and twist dangerously.

Finally the elevator started moving, but all of a sudden it stopped again and no amount of cursing or pressing the buttons seemed to be making them go again.

The grate opened and suddenly Bast's face was -- well, it was really fucking big is what it was -- but it was right there, too.

"Trick? You okay, Sweets?"

"You don't have to shout," he whispered, or at least he tried to, but he was whispering way loud. "I'm right here."

He laughed and slung his arm around Bast's shoulders. "Did anyone ever tell you that you are really fucking pale?"

Bast nodded as they stumbled toward the big bed, the move causing Bast's hair that was -- purple? green? black? blue? -- blue today to tickle his neck. "Yeah, a couple of times. How much did you drink, Sweets? How the hell'd you find your way home?"

"Followed my cock. Missed you." He leaned over and aimed a kiss at Bast's mouth, missing somehow, but Bast's ear was pretty and so that was okay.

"Didn't drink. Wait. Did." He giggled as he remembered the guy with the elaborate nose, ear, eyebrow lip chained together piercing thing. "Rodgy... Doger... Rodjjjj -- Bael's freaky friend brought me one."

"Roger." It was funny, the way Bast could say entire, whole sentences in one word. "The little prick slipped you something, Sweets. Come on, let's get you into bed."

"It's your little prick I want slipping in me." He sat heavily in the bed, bringing Bast down with him. "Only it isn't little." He frowned. "Why would you say your cock was little?"

"To get you to argue with me, of course." Bast laughed and kissed him and made his head spinny.

Oh, he was floating again and this time Bast was with him. He wrapped his arms around his lover's neck and held on, laughing into the kiss. Bast was chuckling with him, holding him, making him stand and twirling him, dancing him to the bed.

Suddenly they were falling back and falling back and floating and Bast was kissing him and he didn't have to worry about being upright or not being upright and everything was just fun and floaty.

Bast nipped and nuzzled, hands nowhere and everywhere all at once, stripping him down to skin. He was covered by a blanket as Bast disappeared. Frowning, he reached for his disappearing lover.

"Gonna get you a glass of water and get undressed, Sweets. I'll be right back. Promise." Dark eyes glittered at him for a second and then faded again.

He let his eyes drop closed, let the colors take over again as he slid his hands along his skin, moaning as they touched off small fireworks.

A soft purring noise sounded as the bed dipped. "Such a beautiful man."

Bast's voice touched him like one of Rose's fur-covered gloves, making him hot and tingly and melty all at once. He arched up as if into the sound, twisting, searching for more of the aural caress.

The chuckle tickled, husky and low, and then Bast's voice slid over him again -- heated oil or silk sheets. "So responsive, Sweets. I love how you move for me, hunt for sensation. Delicious."

"Fuck, yeah. Want to taste you, eat you, feed you." He tried to open his eyes, but the floating turned to swirling and he let them close again.

A long lick to his ear made him shiver, Bast's cool, naked flesh pressing against his side. "My hungry Sweets. You know that I dream of nothing but the splash of your come, your blood upon my tongue? You fill me."

He pressed close to Bast. "I bleed for you, baby-boy."

"I know, my Trick." Soft, full lips covered his, offering him a deep, endless kiss. Bast's hands stroked him, traveling over his belly, his hips, curling around his cock.

Sensation exploded through him, making him shake and scream and the colors behind his eyes went wild; he could feel the climax down to his toes and his fingertips. When the colors faded to a soft grey, Bast was still there, keeping him warm, whispering sweet words that made no sense but meant home and love and ease.

"Everything's moving..." He wasn't sure if it was a complaint or not, but it was beginning to become disconcerting.

"S'okay, Sweets. Roger slipped you something, is all. You'll be okay." Bast closed his eyes with gentle fingers. "Just sleep it off."

"You're hungry," he protested. He could feel it, feel Bast's hunger like an itch beneath his skin.

"Shh... I'm fine, lover." Another kiss, this one almost chaste, soft and honey-sweet. "Last thing we need is for both of us to be high at the same time, right? It would take me two days to come down."

"Two days?" Panic flared in his stomach: he couldn't do this for two days, the rolling and floating that had been fun was becoming too much.

"Hey, hey, Sweets, chill." Bast's voice was calm, relaxed and that helped calm him. "I've got a really slow metabolism, remember? You know, *really* slow? You'll wake up a little groggy tonight. No big deal. Trust me."

He reached out and found Bast's arm, wrapping his hand around it. "You're staying, right?"

"Right here, babe. Nowhere else I'd rather be."

"Okay. Okay, good." He nuzzled against Bast. "Love you, baby-boy."

Bast hummed softly, pulled the comforter over them, holding him close. "I love you, Sweets. Sleep now. I'm right here."

"Ne'er thought of you as a teddy 'ear 'efore."

A soft chuckle floated over his throat. "Yes, Sweets. Your own bloodsucking, kinky little stuffed Sebastian. All the blond studmuffins want one."

"Yeah... I would if I didn't already have one." His own words sounded so far away, Bast's even farther. The floating was slowing, giving way to sinking.

"Yes, Sweets. Sleep." A final, lingering kiss followed him down into dreams.

# Chapter Fifteen

Trick grabbed on end of the divan and began to drag it over to the foot of the bed. He always teased Bast about how it was up on those silly little glass furniture leg coasters, but he had to admit, they sure made it easy to move. He supposed that was the point, but he'd only ever seen them in old people's houses.

Not that he'd been in that many old people's houses and really, Bast was pretty much older than anyone he knew. Not that his lover looked it. And that, after all, was why he was busy moving furniture.

"Having the sudden and unavoidable desire to take up interior decorating or is this the season for vacuuming under the furniture?" Bast leaned up against the wall, jeans unbuttoned and damp, dark shirt hanging open as he towel-dried his hair, a warm, fond smile upon his face.

Trick licked his lips, cock jumping inside his own jeans. Oh, yeah. This was a good idea. He shook his head as he piled cushions onto the couch. "Neither. I just needed a comfortable place to watch."

"Watch? Watch what? You're going to have to strain to see the TV from there, Sweets." Bast stretched, his thin stomach rippling, the so-faint line of dark curls coming into view. "What's on the agenda tonight, then? Monster movies on HBO?"

Trick laughed, eyes hungry on Bast's skin. "Actually I'd say it's more of a cross between monster movies and the Playboy channel."

Bast frowned for a second and then understand lit the dark eyes. "Are you suggesting what I think you are, Sweets?" One hand dropped from his head, slowing trailing down his midsection, before curling over his groin.

"Oh, fuck, yes." Trick licked his lips again and managed to tear his eyes away from Bast's wandering hand. "I want to watch you fuck yourself."

Bast's eyes flashed, the lean body rippling under his gaze. "You have something particular in mind, Sweets? Fingers? Dildo? Appropriately proportioned carrot?" The words were teasing, but the voice husky and more than willing to play.

Trick grinned, suddenly ravenous for Bast, for playing, but he'd set this up as a show, so he had to back off. "Dealer's choice, baby-boy -- whatever you want."

"Mmm... nice and simple then." Bast waggled his fingers and winked over. "This way I'll be ready for you to fuck me when I feed. You want me on the bed or here against the wall?"

"Oh..." He was all set up for the bed, complete with

viewing couch, but where Bast was, leaning up against the wall and half dressed was just about the sexiest thing he'd seen in awhile and it was making his cock hard. He stripped off his jeans and shucked his shirt and climbed into the bed himself. "Up against the wall."

Bast nodded. "Anything you want, Sweets." He grinned at Trick, licking his lips slowly. Leaning heavily, he slid down the cream wall, thighs spreading just enough to make the denim pull tight across his hardening cock. Long, thin hands combed through the shoulder length hair, gleaming black in the low lamplight.

Trick made a soft noise that was almost a whimper and wrapped his hands in the sheets so he didn't touch himself. Bast stretched up, one hand sliding along the doorframe, the other moving down the long, curved throat.

"I imagine sometimes that you are like me, that you need to feed from me." Bast's voice was low and seductive, chocolate-coated desire. "I don't remember what it feels like, to be fed from. I was so young; it was so long ago. But I know how you scream, know how the touch of my teeth make you come. So, sometimes, I imagine your teeth, sharp on my throat."

Trick licked his teeth, letting his tongue linger over his incisors, and a soft groan left him.

Bast's hand continued downward, slipping down torso and stomach, petting and scraping the pale skin, leaving marks that almost immediately disappeared. "I imagine how it would feel, the pulling, the knowledge that my blood was flowing into you, feeding you." Bast's hand slid into his jeans, hips rocking slowly, undulating against the wall.

Trick leaned forward, tongue moving to lick his lips

now. He could practically taste Bast's blood, his cock, his come.

Eyes closed, Bast began to pinch his nipples with his free hand, pulling hard, making himself bite his lips and groan. "God, Sweets, I can't wait to feel you fucking me, taking me hard, filling me."

"Wanna watch first." He said it as much to remind himself as Bast, the urge to go to his lover and fuck him hard against the wall strong.

Bast pushed down the waistband of his jeans, pulling his hard shaft free. He arched into his fist, moaning as his hips moved. The dark, shiny head appeared between Bast's thumb and forefinger with each thrust, the scent of Bast's need slowly traveling across the room. "'s hot, knowing you're watching, knowing you're hot and right there."

"Hot?" Trick asked, his voice shaky. "I'm on fucking fire." He let go of the sheets and let his hands run up and down his thighs, moving in time with Bast's hand.

"Beautiful Sweets... you make me hungry." Eyes opening, Bast's gaze burned across him, flashed golden green at him. Trick could *see* the hunger in the slowing of Bast's hips, the sudden liquid silk of movement, the shift from self-focused pleasure to seduction.

It called to him, found his own hunger and stoked the flame beneath it. He whimpered. Bast wasn't playing fair. Bast stroked his own stomach, his hips, his inner thighs, making soft, hungry noises that on their own seemed insignificant, but together created a melody of desire that seemed to whisper Trick's name. All the while, Bast pumped his cock, thumb moving to slide across the slit with every stroke.

Trick took a deep breath and he swore he could

smell Bast's precome. He dug his nails into his thighs, determined to *watch* until Bast made himself come.

"Mmm... want you, Sweets. Want to feel your cock in my throat. Want to feel you slamming me into the wall. Want to hear your scream, feel your come on me, in me, when I feed from you." A red stain covered Bast's lower belly, his motions becoming jerky and quick. "So hungry, love. Want to make you my heartbeat..." Bast came with a low cry, creamy fluid pulsing over his hand, head falling back against the wall.

Trick grabbed his balls, pulling hard on them to keep himself from coming. Gasping, he watched as Bast slowly came down, waiting to go to his lover, making them both wait. Finally Bast's head lifted, hands pushing the faded jeans down and off, the dark shirt shrugged off. Slowly, eyes glittering at Trick, Bast rubbed his seed into his skin, making him shine softly in the lamplight.

"Fuck." Trick swallowed and licked his lips, breathing heavily. "What do you want, baby-boy? Do you want me to fuck your mouth or your ass?"

"Mmm... choices, choices..." Cock satisfied, Bast was all hunger, sleek and silken and sharp. He undulated as his hands moved over his skin. "I want you to take my ass, Sweets. Hard and fast and deep."

"I think I can manage that." Trick barely recognized his own voice, twisted as it was by hunger and need. His eyes were locked onto Bast's hands, watching them move, watching that body move. His hunger would not be held back much longer.

"Trick, Sweets... I need you. Come and feed me, love."

He shot off the bed, almost leaping across the space between them. Hooking his hands beneath Bast's arms, he dragged his lover up, mouth crushing against Bast's as soon as they were face to face. Pulling those lean legs up around his waist, he pushed, cock searching for the heat he needed.

Bast's lips parted for him, tongue pushing against his steadily. His lover shifted, tilted and pushed down, groaning low and harsh as the tip of his cock slid inside.

"Oh, fuck, you're hot." Trick gasped and pushed the rest of the way in. "And tight."

Bast's eyes were glowing, hunger tangible. "Hard and fast and deep, Sweets. Want to feel you in my bones."

He nodded. "I don't think I could do it any other way, baby-boy. Not with the way you were teasing me."

Trick shifted slightly, getting a better grip and pulled out. Taking a deep breath he gave Bast a wild smile and slammed back in. It was easy to find the rhythm they both wanted and the sound of that sweet body hitting the wall each time he slammed in spurred him on. Bast's arms were hard on his shoulders, legs tight around his waist. For every thrust, Bast pushed back, meeting him, taking everything he gave. The bright eyes never left his face, the lush mouth open and hungry.

His movements became harder, more frantic and jerky. When he couldn't hold out any longer he tilted his head back in mute invitation.

"Sweets..." The whisper against his throat was full of awe and need, brushing softly a mere second before Bast's fang struck deep.

It was always the same; the moment Bast bit into him he lost all control. Pleasure crashed through him, making him scream, making him come. Shudders rocked through him with each suck of Bast's mouth against his skin. He could hear his blood rushing through his veins, imagined he could hear it pushing into Bast's mouth, filling the vampire with himself, come and blood and life mixing together.

Bast was all heat and languid pleasure in his arms, lips easing, the pull slowing and fading by tiny increments. Bast drew it out, giving Trick long, breathless moments of sweet sensation. He was shaking by the time Bast closed the wound and he pulled out gently, mourning their joining with a soft noise and then slid to the ground, his lover still wrapped in his arms. "I love you, baby-boy."

Bast's hands were busy, stroking over his hair, his face, his shoulders, soft kisses pressed to his throat, his jaw. "Oh, Trick, I love you. Was it what you wanted, Sweets? Watching me?"

He chuckled, nuzzling into the sweet touches. "As usual, when it comes to sex you surpass all my expectations."

Bast blinked, nipping sharply at his ear. "Only when it comes to sex?"

Trick laughed, the sound feeling good as it bubbled up his chest. "I knew you were going to say that."

"Of course you did." The bite turned into a warm nuzzle. "You know *me*, Sweets." He turned his face to meet Bast's mouth, the kiss soft and full, unhurried. Bast was warm and heavy, eyelashes brushing against him. "Mm... love you, Sweets."

"I love you, too, Bast. A lot. A scary lot."

Bast gave him another kiss, fingers trailing through his hair, soothing and easy. "So... my Sweets... want to make use of the divan? I mean, you went to all the trouble to move it..."

"You offering to give me another show?"

"I'll give you whatever you want, Sweets." Bast

nibbled again. "Or you could give me one..."

He shuddered, the thought of touching himself while Bast watched almost as arousing as the thought of Bast fucking himself on a fake cock, spread out on the bed, slender body moving...

Another bite, this one hard enough to break the skin. "Or we could do both."

Moaning, he shuddered again. "Both?"

"Mmmhmm. I could watch you while you watch me and then," Nip. "Then I could lick the come off your belly," Nibble. "And then suck you until you're hard again," Long wet lick. "And then have a snack and then we can do it all over again." Bast bit his way to Trick's mouth, taking Trick's lower lip and biting it firmly, sucking the trickle of blood off lazily, savoring it.

Pleasure was zinging through him, making him hard. He reached out with his tongue, meeting and playing with Bast's. "Or you could just keep talking and I'll come all over you."

"Works for me, lover." Bast began rocking in his lap and making soft, purring noises. "I'll take you anyway I can get you. In me, on me, around me. All over me."

Trick swallowed. "If I had to make a picture of what sex looked like, I'd use a picture of you."

"Would you? What about need and heat and want and passion?" Bast took his head between his hands and kissed him deeply, black eyes huge and warm. "And love, my Trick? What about that?"

"Need would be you about to feed. Heat would be you half naked, working on fully naked. Want would be you in seduction mode, you know, when you really pour it on, even though you don't need to because I'm a sure thing. Passion - that would be you arching, reaching up for my touch." He nibbled on Bast's lips, licking and sucking and letting his teeth sink into the soft flesh. "And love..." He looked into Bast's eyes and then smiled slowly and raised one of his wrists. He traced the barely visible thin white scar at the main artery, knew there were others on his body -- his neck, the inside of his thighs, his ankles, his cock. "This is love."

"Oh. My Trick." Bast's eyes flashed, fingers trembling upon his cheeks. "Yes. This... all of it... our love."

He nodded, feeling like a sap and not really caring. "I know I say it's like a drug, needing to feed you, but that's not quite it, is it? It's love existing inside and outside of you."

"It's life, Trick. You inside me, living and beating and breathing." Bast shuddered, an ageless hunger shining from his eyes. "Want to know a secret? I can feel you, inside me, heat and hope and love. Never before. I have never felt that before." Bast leaned forward for a kiss. "Never before."

Trick choked back a sob and wrapped Bast in a tight hug, holding him close. What was between them was so much and it scared him sometimes: the night he'd come back to Bast, the first time he'd said I love you, this.

And this time, like every time, Bast curled around him and held on, lips and hands and body protecting and loving him. He held on until he'd stopped shaking, until the overwhelming nature of what they shared faded into the background, leaving behind the simpler joys of bodies touching, needing, wanting.

Bast was nibbling on his collarbone, dragging his teeth along the skin, setting the nerves to sparking. He made a happy purring noise and stretched slightly, skin sliding against Bast's. "So what do you want to do, baby-boy?"

Bast continued his nipping, humming happily. "We could take this to the bed, make love until morning. Or in the shower, although the floor's hard there, too."

"Bed. Only we make love until tomorrow night and then you can pour me into my clothes and take me out for a great big, bloody steak."

"Sounds perfect, Sweets." Bast kissed him again before untangling their bodies and standing.

Trick spent a moment just looking up, admiring the view from the floor. He grinned and held out his hand. "Personification of sex, I swear."

"Mm... you just like my ass." Bast helped him up and then sauntered to the bed, hips swaying.

"Oh, I do indeed." He watched said ass move until Bast was almost at the bed and then he pounced, bringing them both down onto the tangle of sheets.

Bast laughed, the sound warm and happy, and then Trick found himself flipped onto his back, Bast straddling his thighs and grinning down, fangs flashing. "If we're lucky, you'll need two steaks in the morning."

Grinning, Trick bucked up, pushing his hips up hard. "And if you're very good, I'll need three."

"Oh, I can be very, very good, Sweets. With appropriate motivation, of course."

"I think I can find appropriate motivation..."

Bast's hands wrapped around his cock, fangs flashing. "I have no doubt."

Arms spreading wide, Trick lay back and let Bast love him into oblivion.

# Chapter Sixteen

Bast hadn't intended to do it -- he'd done it before, but not lately and it hadn't even been on his mind -- but Trick was watching a movie and he was bored and itchy and needed a shower.

So, Bast had stripped himself down and hopped in, steaming hot water beating down on him, the smell of soap and shampoo everywhere. He'd been perfectly content.

Then he'd caught a glimpse of Trick's razor.

He'd grabbed it, amused himself with the shocky, sparkly edge against his inner arm and the itchy, bug-crawling feel of knitting flesh for a bit until that got boring, too. Idly, not quite ready to leave the warm pleasure of the water, he began to shave the tiny line of black-black hair beneath his navel.

Felt pretty fucking good, actually.

So, he grabbed the soap and continued, slowly scraping away the ebony curls, exposing pale skin never touched by the sun. By the time he was done assuring himself that he was completely smooth, the water was cooling and he could hear Trick's laughter at whatever he was watching carrying through the walls, tempting him out.

Kissing a laughing Trick was quite entertaining.

It didn't take him long to dry and smooth on some lotion -- Trick might tease, but his Sweets liked the smooth softness of his skin, liked touching him, so Bast moisturized. Besides, he thought with a chuckle, he had great elasticity for a man of his age.

Throwing on a short, silky, black robe, he grabbed a towel for his hair and went in to settle next to Trick on the bed. "Enjoying the movie, Sweets?"

Nodding, eyes still on the screen, Trick reached over and slid a hand around Bast's thigh, the touch at once casual and possessive. "Adam Sandler's an idiot, but he makes me laugh."

Bast studied Trick's hand, thick and square and strong. He stroked over the knuckles, chuckling as Trick's fingers tightened on his leg. "Does that tickle?"

This time Trick shook his head and shifted closer. "Feels good."

"Yeah, it does." Bast continued the soft touches, leaning over to rest his head against the small of Trick's back, thigh turning beneath Trick's hand. "You always feel good."

"Mmm..." Trick's hand rubbed absently along his thigh.

Bast half-dozed, cheek pillowed against Trick's body, humming softly as the warm hand traveled, stroking and petting. He was almost fully asleep, woken only now and then by Trick's chuckles, when the square fingers moved beneath his robe to stroke against his newly bare skin. Trick's hand stuttered and returned, fingers wide and questing; they stuttered again when they found his half-hard cock and his bared balls.

"What?"

"'s my crotch, Sweets." Bast grinned against Trick's skin, pleased with his lover's reaction. "I know you remember it. You saw it up and close and personal just last night."

Trick chuckled. "I know it's your crotch, Bast, but it wasn't naked last night." Trick shifted and pushed him onto his back, hands sliding apart his robe. "Would you look at that..."

Bast shifted and stretched, legs sliding together smoothly, letting Trick look his fill. "You like?"

"Yeah, it's fucking hot." Trick reached out and slid a finger along the bared skin, eyes riveted. He grinned suddenly and his eyes were twinkling, pupils dilated wide with pleasure. "Makes your cock look bigger, too."

Bast chuckled, hips automatically following the movement of Trick's finger. "Does it? Hard to believe shaving a few dark hairs makes a difference." The look of pleased interest caused his cock to twitch and firm as it worked to keep Trick's attention.

"Yeah, well see your cock used to look like it went down to here." Trick's finger circled the base of his cock, about an inch from his balls. "But without all those curls, you can tell it goes right down to here." This time Trick's finger went down to slid against the skin right above his balls.

He purred happily, pushing up into the sensation. He

let his thighs part, let his fingers move to slide over his torso, knowing he looked hungry and wanton and erotic. Knowing Trick would love it.

Moaning, Trick shifted and stretched his legs out behind him, lying with his chest resting between Bast's legs, his head level with the newly bared skin. Trick dipped his head and licked along the sensitized flesh.

"Oh!" Trick's tongue was hot, hotter than Bast had expected, leaving bright tingles behind it and Bast half-sat up, shuddering. "Fuck, Sweets! That feels... Do it again?"

A soft chuckle sent air skittering over his wet flesh, raining goose bumps. "Try and stop me." This time Trick used just the very tip of his tongue to dance over his skin

"St...stop you? Why would I... oh, fuck, that's good, right there... why would I do that?" Bast eased back against the bed, moaning softly beneath the hot, wet touches that seemed to burn into him.

The hot, wet touches continued, sometimes long licks, other times short, teasing flicks with the tip of Trick's tongue. His cock was throbbing, fingers pulling and plucking his nipples in concert with Trick's tongue. The pace was lazy, the hunger and desire building in steady stages, making him hot and hungry and hard.

Suddenly, Trick moaned and buried his face in Bast's crotch, nose dragging over the sensitive skin as he breathing in deeply. "You smell great."

"Oh..." So sexy, so fucking erotic -- his hands moved to twist into the blond hair, petting the heavy silken strands. "Sweets."

"Mm." Trick moved his head back and forth, nose sliding along the new skin. "Makes me want to eat you up." Mouth opening wide, Trick let his teeth scrape over

Bast's skin. Bast gave a short, sharp cry, hips thrusting up, heels digging into the mattress. "Oh, you like that, do you?" The words were his only warning before Trick grabbed a mouthful of skin and closed his teeth over it in a sharp bite.

"Fuck!"

Trick chuckled and let the skin go. "Oh, I plan to, baby-boy, but you're going to have to be patient, I'm having fun down here."

Moving to the other side of Bast's cock, Trick took another inch of the bared skin between his lips and bit. Every muscle tensed with the intense sensation, his cock aching, leaking against his belly. Bast rode the pleasure-pain, gasping and shaking at the touch of Trick's teeth.

"I love the new look," Trick told him as he shifted, moving to lap at the drops coming from his cock.

"Do you?" He sobbed softly, twisting, trying to get closer to that hungry mouth.

"Uh-huh." The tip of Trick's tongue slid along his cock to his balls, circling them each. Trick kept moving down though, nosing against the sensitive patch of skin behind his balls. The scrape of teeth threatened and then Trick bit him again.

His scream echoed through the room, hands gripping the base of his cock as his orgasm threatened. "Oh, fuck... Sweets, God, you're gonna make me... fuck, Trick. Please..."

Trick's nose nudged against his balls, tongue sliding over the abused flesh. "What, Bast? Please what?"

"More, Sweets. Fuck me." Bast lifted his head, forcing his eyes open. "Want to feel you, Trick. Please."

Trick was looking up at him, eyes glittering, licking his lips. Then his Sweets shifted again, sitting back on his heels and slowly opening his jeans, making a tease of it. Pushing aside the open flaps of the black pants, Trick freed his cock and began to stroke it. "Is this what you want to feel, baby-boy?"

"Fuck, yes." He was shivering, hunger creeping up along his spine. Bast pushed the hunger away, focusing on his need, his desire, the empty ache in his belly that wanted to be filled. Bast spread his legs further, inviting, pleading.

"Just like that, baby-boy? I'm not even undressed yet. And the lube's still way over there." All the while he spoke, Trick's hand moved in long, lazy strokes over his own cock. Trick's hands slid down over his balls, cupping them, fingers trailing over the so-sensitive bite mark. He groaned, hips pushing up rhythmically.

"Trick... Sweets... Need you." He let the edges of his hunger show, let it out to tempt his lover closer.

"You really want it, don't you? Really want to feel me inside you, hot and hard and just as hungry as you?"

"Always." He stopped writhing, stilled and looked steadily at Trick, love and lust and need and sweet hunger filling him. "Always, Trick."

"You want it like it is, or do you want me to get you ready first?" Question after question and still Trick stroked his own erection, hand moving slowly, lazily, as if he had all the time in the world.

"Trick..." Bast growled, fingers sliding back and forth over the bite mark. "Quit teasing and fuck me."

"Anything you want, baby-boy. Anything." With that Trick leaned forward, arms sliding beneath Bast's legs, cock pushed against his entrance.

"Yes..." He bore down against Trick's cock, groaning at the burning stretch as the hard flesh pressed inside his body.

Trick pushed in until the zipper of his jeans bit into Bast's flesh. It burned, but it felt good -- deep and right, satisfying his need to be touched, to be filled and felt. Trick's arms came down on either side of his head, Trick's hair falling against his face as his lover looked down at him and began to move. He reached up and wrapped his arms around Trick's neck, fingers sliding through Trick's hair. He held on tight, body moving in the rhythm they found so easily, so naturally.

"Sweets. Good. So fucking good."

"Yeah, baby-boy, going to fuck you good." Trick laugh was husky and full of heat.

"Can you do it any other way?" He leaned up and took a hard kiss, nipping Trick's bottom lip sharply and lapping at the stain of blood. Trick shuddered but didn't lose the rhythm, thrusting fast and hard.

Bast rode wave after wave of pleasure, the pressure and stroke of Trick's cock driving him higher and higher, his body shivering with need and pleasure. A drop of sweat slid along Trick's cheek and chin and from there dropped down with a splash against his skin.

He could feel Trick's heartbeat in the cock inside him, keeping time with each thrust. Trick's blood called to him, sliding through the veins beneath his sweet's flushed skin.

He leaned in, hunger mingling with passion and becoming need, nuzzling Trick's throat. The flat of his tongue tasted the throbbing pulse, body and hunger tight as a bow. "Trick... now, Sweets? Now?"

"Take what you need, baby-boy."

"My life." The whisper was harsh and heartfelt, his body convulsing as his teeth sank into Trick's throat and he drank greedily, savoring the flavor of his lover.

Trick's scream of pleasure was familiar, as much a part of this as his fangs. Heat filled him, Trick's seed joining the blood in his body, bringing him heat and life. He suckled for a long time, lost in the flavor and scent and feel of Trick in him, on him, through him. Finally Trick began to sag against him and he closed the wound, purring softly against Trick's throat, sated within and without.

Trick settled on him heavily. "Love you, Bast."

He wrapped around his lover, arms and legs, holding Trick close. "Me, too, Sweets."

Nuzzling against him, Trick murmured indistinctly.

He dropped a soft kiss against Trick's temple before settling back, floating and warm and happy.

# Chapter Seventeen

Trick was brushing his hair, watching himself in the mirror. Bast stepped slowly, silently, keeping well behind so he could watch. Look. Admire.

Pretty Sweets.

Trick checked the ends and muttered something about them getting long. Bast leaned forward, blowing a soft stream of air between Trick's shoulder blades. Trick shivered, eyes looking for him in the mirror.

Bast grinned and blew again, slowly kneeling. Trick shivered again, glancing over his shoulder but not looking down. He breathed out, almost touching Trick's lower back.

A ripple moved up Trick's body. "Baby-boy?"

Bast smiled, tongue pressing at the top of Trick's cleft.

Trick groaned. "You know who you are? What's the

name of that trickster god, again?"

"Which one, Chosen? There are so many..." He spread Trick's legs, hands sliding up, tongue sliding down.

"Fuck if I know. I can't see you in the mirror, but I know you're there." Trick leaned forward a little, hands on the counter, legs spreading further for him.

"Mmm... Are you sure?" He lapped at Trick's hole, purring softly.

Trick made a choking noise. "Hell of a... of a hallucination."

He chuckled and let his teeth slide around Trick's skin.

A shudder moved through his Sweets. "Oh, baby-boy, you gonna feed?"

He purred and licked again, teasing, taunting, teeth close.

"Tease," Trick accused, pushing back, trying to get him to bite.

He could see Trick's neck in the mirror, his Sweets' head thrown back in pleasure and need. He kept licking, kept nuzzling and lapping and driving his Chosen higher. That sweet prick was jerking, reaching up for Trick's belly and leaving wet kisses on the lovely skin. Mmm... Wet kisses. He fucked Trick with his tongue, trying to keep his hunger in check.

"Oh fuck. Bast... please." Trick whimpered eyes on the mirror, despite the fact Bast didn't have a reflection.

He pressed between Trick's legs, nuzzling the soft balls for only a second before dropping his mouth down over Trick's cock, biting deep at the base. Blood and come filled his mouth, Trick's scream of pleasure in his ears. He fed, pulling life and sex and need and Trick into him.

Trick's hand dropped to his head, fingers wrapping in

his hair, holding him in place. The screams had turned to soft, pleasure-filled whimpers. Life filled him, their hearts pounding together and it was only reluctantly that he closed the wounds, licking gently.

Trick was shaking, hands white against the counter. “Oh, baby-boy. Love you. Love you, so much.”

He nuzzled, purring. “Chosen.”

Trick looked down, smiling at him, eyes half dazed and full of love.

He slid up, pushing into Trick’s arms, tongue sliding over those parted lips. “Mine.”

Trick wrapped around him. “Yeah. But you’re mine, so we’re even.”

He chuckled and nodded, grinning wide. “We should get a mirror above the bed. You could watch yourself.”

“I don’t know... it would be kind of weird.”

Bast tilted his head. “Yes, and then you wouldn’t be watching me.”

“Well we can’t have that, baby-boy.”

“No. No, we can’t have that at all.”

Not at all.

# Chapter Eighteen

One of the best parts about dancing with Trick was the teasing.

Bast loved the chase, the rubbing, the beat. The alcohol and the sweat and the stolen kisses. The press of bodies. The flowing clothes that hid a tight black corset and nipple clamps.

It was all good.

He turned toward Trick, flashing open his huge coat before sidling away.

Oh, that shocked his Sweets. Trick actually stopped dancing for a moment, eyes hard on him as if just by staring hard enough Trick could see through his coat. Then his Sweets picked up the beat and started dancing again, a little more of a slink in each movement.

He grinned, leaned back into the arms of some big guy, eyes still on Trick, playing, teasing. Trick moved slowly toward him, staying with the music, eyes almost glowing preternaturally, nostrils flaring as if his Sweets could smell him.

Oh, he loved being hunted.

Bast turned, rubbed against the pretty, big man, then moved on, kissing a little girl with blue eyes, spinning between a couple, daring Trick to catch him. He looked back, watched as Trick slid against the same big man and kissed the wee slip of a thing with the big eyes. Trick's eyes never left him though, not for a second.

He felt his hunger flare suddenly, unexpectedly, and he lowered his eyes as he went feral and knew they'd gone gold. His Trick knew though, the music suddenly left behind as his Sweets hurried toward him. Bast threw his head back, body tight, wanting, the laugh that escaped him almost a cry.

Trick walked right into him, arms going around him, pulling him up tight against all those warm muscles. "Baby-boy." Trick's voice was a growl, needy, possessive.

"Chosen." He pushed in, hips rocking, baring his teeth, letting Trick see his hunger.

Trick looked around, eyes searching. "There's a door near the back marked private."

"Private is good. Need you." He licked Trick's throat, nuzzling close.

"I know. I can feel it. Feel you." Trick's voice was strained and he could feel the hard cock pressing against him through his coat.

They moved toward the door, dancing, hips bumping together, grinding. It seemed to take for damned ever, but at last they were at the door and Trick breathed a huge sigh as the door proved not to be locked. They stumbled in, Trick pressing him against the wall, his ass rubbing against Trick's cock.

"Want you, baby-boy. Need you like a drug." Trick's voice was rough, hands pulling his coat off.

"Yours." He purred, stretching under Trick's hands, toes curling.

"Look at you..." Trick turned him, hands sliding over his skin through the corset.

He wiggled, preening, knowing how good he looked, how the corset made him seem otherworldly and sensuous. "You like, Sweets?"

"You know I do." Trick's mouth descended on his, tongue invading as his Sweets pushed him up against the wall again, pressing close. He purred into the kiss, fingers pushing into Trick's thick hair, leg wrapping around Trick's thigh. Yes. Yes, he knew.

Trick drew back suddenly. "You've got nipple clamps on!"

"So observant, Sweets." He winked, grinning wide.

"Wicked, sexy beast." Trick's finger slid against one of his clamped nipples. He arched into the touch, shivering just a little.

Trick moaned, hips pressing against his, pushing him into the wall again and again as warm fingers explored and teased. He nipped at Trick's lips, tongue stealing away the scant drops of blood that he drew.

Trick shuddered, rocking harder. "Bast... please."

Bast chuckled, biting harder, sucking Trick's bottom lip.

Another shudder worked through his Sweets. "Tease," Trick accused.

"Mmmhmm." His fingers tickled their way down to cup Trick's cock, hold it.

His Sweets growled and rubbed against his hand,

fingers hitting the clamps making them wiggle on his nipples. That, in turn, made him jerk, made his eyes roll, sent lines of sensation down his belly.

"You gonna feed, baby-boy?" It wasn't really a question; it was more a plea.

"Think I need to, Chosen. Hungry." He bared his teeth, nuzzled into Trick's neck and inhaled, breathing Trick in.

Whimpering, Trick pressed closer, one hand going up to the back of his neck, holding him there. "Please, Bast. Please."

He opened Trick's jeans, fingers wrapping around the hot flesh as he bit deep, pleasure and need bringing him to his toes.

Trick's scream drowned out the music, heat pouring out over his hands, over his lips and teeth. He fed until he was sated, trapping his Chosen in a web of pure pleasure, binding them together.

Trick leaned against him, gasping and shuddering as he closed the puncture marks.

"Mmm...taste good, Sweets. Like life."

Trick smiled at him, looking happy and sated, good. "Love you, baby-boy."

He licked at Trick's mouth, chuckling. " Chosen."

Trick rubbed against him. "You want to go back out there and dance up a storm? Work up another appetite?"

Bast nodded, happy and full, sensing the beat again. "Come play with me, Sweets."

# Chapter Nineteen

If Rose or Bael had come down the elevator, they wouldn't have recognized him -- hair pulled back, pair of faded jeans and one of Trick's old t-shirts on, bare footed and lying on the floor, typing intently. Completely engrossed in his work, Bast had been working for weeks, finishing up a project that his sister, of all people, had found for him.

Trick had gone out earlier, muttering something about being cooped up. Bast sighed as he typed up a line of code and ran the simulator again. He and Trick hadn't gone out, hadn't had sex, hadn't done much of anything except sleep in the same bed in well over two weeks. He hadn't even fed from Trick in... three days? Four? Not a week; he couldn't go *that* long.

Damn this project and his sister and her promises anyway. Bast sighed, shifting around and then dove back into the oceans of code. He'd just get it finished and be done with it.

He had no idea how long he'd been working when the sounds of the elevator warned him that someone was coming. Hitting save, he turned in time to see Trick opening the grate, though he had to look twice to be sure it *was* Trick.

His Sweets was wearing leather pants that were quite possibly two sizes too small and a leather vest. His hair was, well, styled, and streaked with gold and bronze and silver. Most startling of all was the tattoo: a single tear-shaped drop of blood beneath Trick's left eye.

"Sweets?" Fuck, but he looked good -- sex and energy and predatory hunger that no human should carry off as well as Trick did. Bast shivered, cock going hard, body remembering that there were hungers that needed to be satisfied.

Trick strode toward him, hips leading, arms swinging casually. He stopped at Bast's feet, hands going to his hips. Bast could feel the heat pouring from him. Trick stared down at him; the blood drop looked fresh, raw, real.

Bast rolled over and sat up, hands reaching to slide up the leather-covered legs. He could smell Trick -- heat and sex and leather and... "Fuck, you're beautiful. You make me ache."

"I wondered what it would take to get your attention." Trick didn't move, simply stood over him, "It's not a tattoo, you know. It's a cut. He put a piece of clear tape on it so it would stop bleeding. If it's not taken care of, it's going to leave a scar."

"A cut?" Hunger flashed through him, rich and wild and undeniable. "Why?"

"Why?" Trick laughed a little hysterically. "Because I've been all but invisible around here -- can you even remember the last time you fed from me, baby-boy?" Trick's hand went to his face, finger picking at the edge of the tape.

"Oh, Sweets..." He leaned forward, nuzzling at Trick's groin for a moment before standing and pressing close to his lover. "I'm sorry, love. I've just... that stupid project..." His excuses and apologies were derailed by the scent of blood so close.

Trick's fingers tore away the tape, the blood welling immediate in the tear-shaped cut. "You can't find a few minutes now and then to feed? You know when you get hungry; you can always heat up a bag of blood. I've been left with nothing -- *nothing* -- for six days, fourteen hours and thirty seven minutes."

"Six..." Bast stretched up, rubbing against Trick's body with a growl. His tongue slid against Trick's cheek, the dark, sweet taste of blood teasing him.

Trick's arms came around him, grabbing at his ass and pulling him tight against the hard body. Trick's cock was like steel inside the leather, hard and hot.

Bast twined around his lover, rocking against Trick's body, tongue searching out more of that addictive flavor. "More... need more. Fuck, Sweets, you make me hungry."

Trick was shaking, tiny tremors that he probably wouldn't have noticed if they hadn't been so close. "Then feed, baby-boy, please..."

He looked into Trick's eyes, he could see his own need reflected within them. "I love you."

He took a long, slow kiss, enjoying the flavor of his lover's mouth. Then he slid his lips down, tongue finding the quick beat of Trick's pulse, and waited, drawing out the anticipation. Trick sobbed, hands coming up to press him against the warm neck. Trick's shudders were growing more pronounced, heart beat beginning to race.

He bit, unable and unwilling to wait. Blood filled him as he pulled strongly at the wound, heat and sweetness and rich dark overwhelming need singing through his body. Trick jerked against him, his scream immediate and long. The hands in Bast's hair held him tightly in place, even as Trick began to sob in time with each suck.

Bast rubbed himself against Trick as he fed, moaning softly, cock aching as his belly filled. His hands held Trick close, fingers tangled in Trick's hair.

"Love you, Bast." Trick's words were soft, his hands gentling in Bast's hair as he began to grow weaker, his need to feed Bast sated, his body growing heavy. Bast slowly closed the wound, laying his tongue against Trick's throat for a long moment. It felt so good, Trick's heat against him, within him, all through him.

"Thank you."

"Shh... I should have paid more attention, should have stopped earlier." Bast nuzzled into Trick's throat, purring softly at the feel and smell of his Sweets. "You should kick me next time. Hard."

Trick snorted and kissed his head, arms looping around his waist. "Make love to me, Bast?"

"Yes, Sweets." Bast slowly walked them over to the bed, hands working upon the laces of Trick's vest and pants, tongue licking softly against salt-sweet skin. "My beautiful love."

"I'm not sure I'm ever going to get out of these now that I've come in them." Trick shook his head. "Nothing else seemed to work though." Trick closed Bast's mouth with warm lips, kissing him deeply. "The cut on my face aches; can you kiss it better?"

"Mmm... my pleasure." Bast kissed his way up Trick's cheek, licking and tasting, closing the wound with ease. He continued licking Trick's cheek, tracing the new, pink flesh with his tongue.

Trick shuddered softly, purring, hands tracing random patterns along Bast's back. Bast slowly began to lick and suck his way down Trick's jaw, hands removing the leather vest and then working to open the tight pants. He whispered soft endearments against Trick's skin, each word a spell, a promise, a hope.

Trick's hands moved through his hair, caressing his scalp slowly, making soft sounds of pleasure and love. "Missed you so much, baby-boy."

"Missed you, Sweets." His lips were fascinated by the contrasts of texture between the hollows of Trick's collarbones and the curve of strong shoulders. "God, you taste so good, so good."

"That's need you taste, Bast. And want and hunger and anticipation and desire that've been lingering for six days..."

He swooped up, stealing Trick's words with his mouth, before grinning widely. "But you taste as good if I've made love to you every minute for six days, Sweets. If I've just sucked you, just fed from you. You just taste good, love."

"Mmm, making love every minute for six days. I like the sound of that." Trick's hands slid to cup his cheeks and brought their mouths back together. "How long until this infernal project of yours is done and we can see if you can keep it up for six days?"

"I could be finished tonight, if I was willing to deny

myself your sweet body." Bast shrugged, hands pushing the leather off Trick's hips. "I'll finish tomorrow."

"Oh, good." Trick made a face. "Fuck, I'm a mess."

"Want to come shower with me?"

"If by 'shower with you' you mean fuck you under the spray of hot water, hell yes."

"Oh, wonderful." He bent and nibbled at Trick's collarbone. "I can survive if I don't have you, but once I have the taste of you on my lips... I *need*, Trick."

Trick chuckled. "So you're saying what I should have done was cut my finger and push it into your mouth?"

Bast shivered. "That would have done it, yes. I... I don't look because I want you so... I could get lost in you." He wouldn't look up, buried his face in Trick's belly, breathing in the scent of sex and hunger.

"You mean the way I'm already lost in you?" Trick's voice was rough with hunger, his hands less gentle now as they slid through his hair.

Bast moaned, tongue sliding over Trick's skin, finding the salty evidence of pleasure. The air felt charged, as if he had been half-asleep for days and days and only now came alive.

A moan drifted down, Trick's hips shifting restlessly. "We're not going to make it to the shower, baby-boy."

"No?" He loved the skin of Trick's sac, velvet and warmth beneath his lips.

"Fuck, no." The words were almost growled and Trick was pushing him back against the bed.

Bast groaned, reaching for Trick, lips refusing to leave the sweet skin. Trick kept pushing until Bast's mouth slid over his cock. Whimpering, he began to move his hips, sliding in and out of Bast's mouth. This was better than feeding, better than anything -- Bast moaned, sucking firmly on Trick's cock, each new slide of flavor making him ache and shudder.

Trick moved faster, harder, thrusting into his mouth, hips snapping urgently. With a gasp, Bast swallowed Trick deep, using his strength to hold Trick still as he bit the base of the thick cock. Trick made a noise somewhere between a grunt, a sob and a laugh, come and blood flooding Bast's mouth.

Bast suckled gently, not taking too much, just enough to satisfy his hunger and send Trick floating. It was bliss -- the taste of Trick upon his tongue. Sheer, complete bliss. Trick was murmuring, slurring words that made no sense, but sounded like love and happy and right. One of Trick's hands slid against his cheek, stroking, touching.

That made him purr happily, easing the intensity of his suction as Trick's cock softened. He nuzzled up against Trick's belly, happy through and through.

"Love you." The words started against his cheek in Trick's belly and then drifted down from Trick's mouth to his ears.

He let his own love sound in his hum, in the stroke of his fingers and the slide of his tongue upon silken flesh. Carefully he settled Trick on his side, crawling up his lover's body to share a sweet, lazy kiss. "I love you."

Trick's arms circled him, limbs heavy. "So good, baby-boy."

"Mm... yeah. There's nothing like you, not anywhere, not ever." Bast pulled away long enough to pull off his jeans and borrowed t-shirt and then pushed close again, sighing happily as Trick's fingers touched him.

"You still gonna be here when I wake up?"

"Where else would I be, Sweets?" He kissed Trick's throat. "I'm where I belong."

"Mm." Trick pulled him closer. "Good."

His eyes fell closed as he melted into his lover.

The laptop blinked silently until the battery ran low and it shut itself off.

# Chapter Twenty

Trick lay spread eagle in the middle of Rose and Bear's big bed. He was bound, wrists and ankles, gag keeping him silent, leather tight around the base of his cock, his balls, keeping him hard.

There had to be at least thirty people in the small apartment, maybe more. Some he knew, most he didn't. He could feel their eyes on him, all of them, even the ones who'd separated out into couples and triples and quadruples, fucking in various corners.

He'd arrived at six, which was when Rose had told him to be here. It was just her and him then, and she'd grinned and tied him to the bed. The others had arrived slowly over the next three hours, each one coming over to look at him, walk around the bed as if he were a centerpiece, before joining the party.

No one had touched him, though many had told him,

in explicit detail, what they wanted to do to him.

Rose had disappeared after the first hour, though he could see her bald head now and then through the crowd, as well as Bael's dark skin.

Of Bast there had been no sign.

Physically, he was comfortable, Rose had seen to that, but he wasn't entirely comfortable with the situation, with being the center of attention. Rose hadn't exactly told him what to expect. He hadn't asked; he had assumed she would tie him up, the usual suspects would turn up for an orgy, and that Bast would be among them. He knew his lover was supposed to be here at some point.

This felt... like he was a part of a show, but he hadn't been given the script. Everybody was watching him and waiting. He breathed deeply through his nose; it was what they might be waiting for that had him nervous.

A soft gasp sounded and the room seemed to almost flutter, a small group of people amassing around the door. He saw Rose and Bael hurry to the middle of the throng, voices murmuring softly. Trick pulled at his bonds, tried to crane his head to see, but he was held fast. He couldn't even call out to ask what was going on, the rubber ball in his mouth allowed for soft sounds to pass, but not words. It was frustrating.

The crowd broke apart, the lights dimming, the music rumbling heavy through the room.

A cool touch stroked across the bottom of his foot, hand wrapping around his ankle in a move that was at once lazy and possessive. "Well, well. What do we have here?"

Bast.

The sound of his lover's voice, his touch, his presence, all served to make Trick relax and grow tense at the same time. Whatever was going on in Rose's warped brain, it was show time.

Bast wandered up alongside the bed, hand sliding up his leg, his hip, his belly, his upper arm. Dark eyes glittered down at him, slightly concerned, slightly aroused. Bast leaned down, brushing a soft kiss against his cheek. "Hey, Sweets. You comfortable? Okay?"

He nodded slightly, wishing he could kiss his lover, needing the connection; he hadn't been touched in hours, just left lying there, naked, hard, noticed, watched, but not touched.

Bast's hands slid over his skin, Bast's eyes focused on his. It was different with Bast here; the hands on his skin weren't doing to him, they were doing for him.

"I don't like the gag, Rose. Take it off." Bast's eyes never left his. There was an edge to the words that spoke volumes. Rose said something Trick couldn't hear and Bast's eyes flared. "I didn't ask you, mijita. Take it off him now."

Trick could see Rose in his periphery, but his eyes never left Bast's as her fingers pulled at the gag, sliding it none too gently from around his head.

He gasped as it came off, opening and closing his mouth and sliding his jaw from side to side. His mouth was dry.

"That's better." Bast leaned down and kissed him thoroughly, licking and tasting, hands sliding over his cock. "You're all dry, Sweets. Want some water?"

Oh, it felt good, Bast's mouth on his, the connection between them electric, wonderful, right. He nodded, not trusting his voice. Bast didn't leave his side, sitting carefully on the bed and pouring a glass of water. A strong hand tilted his head and he was offered a long, cool drink. He swallowed gratefully, finishing the glass without taking a breath. He smiled his thanks up at his lover, keeping his eyes on Bast, pretending they were alone.

"There. Now, let's see if that's better." Bast leaned down and took another long, slow kiss, making his head swim, making the other people fade away until there was only the slide of Bast's tongue, the stroke of Bast's hands, the shine of those eyes and the slow rhythm of the music.

He could feel his own heartbeat in his skin, Bast's touch seeming to draw his blood to the surface, warming him, making his skin sensitive to even the air flowing across it. He whimpered softly into Bast's mouth. Those lips left his, returning again and again for deep, wet kisses, as if Bast was as mesmerized as he was.

Finally, Bast sat back, eyes bright and hot. "Much better, I'd say."

He smiled and gave Bast another nod. Let Rose see that he didn't need to be gagged to keep quiet. The hands on his skin moved restlessly, randomly, Bast watching his face with a warm, pleased little smile.

Bael walked up and nudged Bast with his hip. "Our Trick does leather well, don't you think?"

"*My* Trick, beautiful, but he wasn't being well cared for. You know better."

Trick's gaze flicked across to Bael, catching the chagrined look. "It's Rose's show, I've only been watching from the sidelines."

"She knows better, too." Bast eased his words with a smile. "I do appreciate the gift, though. He's lovely. I'm the envy of the room."

Bast's words brought back into sharp focus that they were in a roomful of people, people who were watching them, staring at him as he lay naked, tied down. Somehow, with Bast there, the entire dynamic changed.

Trick wanted them to watch now, he wanted them to see how Bast could make him writhe and squirm and respond to each touch. He wanted them to understand that it wasn't Bast they should be envying.

Bast's fingers found one of his nipples and began to work it -- not hurting, not pinching hard, but playing, bringing it to a point and then sliding over the tip again and again. All the while, his lover made small talk with Bael.

Somehow Bast managed to look like he wasn't paying attention to Trick at all while letting Trick know without a shadow of a doubt that he was completely and utterly focused. Trick shuddered and bit his lip to keep from crying out, to keep from begging for more.

Suddenly, so quickly Trick wasn't sure he'd seen anything, Bast swooped down and bit his nipple, breaking the skin and then licking the wound closed almost too fast for Trick to feel.

Almost.

A sweet tingle raced along his body, just beneath his skin; if his cock hadn't been all trussed up, he might have come. As it was he shivered, arms and legs jerking against his bonds.

Bast licked his blood-coated lips as he sat back up. "You are sweet. You make me hungry." One hand dropped to stroke lazily against Trick's cock. He nodded frantically, hips pushing up into the languid touches. Bast leaned forward, nibbling at his ear. "Easy, Sweets. I'll take care of you. Just let yourself feel -- I'll feed soon enough and we'll both fly."

He let his eyes close and took a couple of deep

breaths. He narrowed his focus once again to just Bast, to the feelings rushing through him. When he felt more in control he opened his eyes again, automatically searching out Bast's gaze.

"By all the dying gods, you are beautiful." Bast's eyes were glowing softly, fangs just visible as he bit at his bottom lip. Dark hair fell around his face, softening his hard edges, his sharp cheeks and jaw. "I could touch you forever."

It made him smile, made him lick his lips, made him want to come, but he couldn't so he just rode out the sweet pleasure Bast's words filled him with. He felt wanton and sexy and eager.

Bast leaned down, licking along Trick's collarbone. "All these people wish they were me. They all want to touch you, taste you, but they can't. I don't feel like sharing today." Golden eyes met his. "And even if they touched your skin, they couldn't really touch you. I have you running in my veins, Sweets."

A soft moan made it past his lips, a long, delicious shudder shaking his body at Bast's words.

"I can taste you, dark chocolate and whiskey and sex under my tongue."

He whimpered and licked his lips. He could feel each breath gasping in and out of his lungs, the slightest hint of Bast's flavor coloring the air; it had to be much sharper for the vampire.

Bast leaned down and traced Trick's lips with his tongue, nipping gently, tugging with careful teeth. He let his own tongue slide out to caress the sharp points of Bast's incisors, a sweet shudder of arousal passing through him.

The lights dimmed further, the driving music changing

to something slow and slinky. The air was filled with moans and sighs, the smell of leather and oil and sex pervasive.

Bast pressed close, rubbing against him, the brush of clothes maddening against his sensitized skin. Each breath was used to make small sounds of pleasure and need. He pulled futilely against his bonds, wanting to hold Bast, both frustrated and further aroused that he couldn't.

Sharp teeth scraped against his throat, tongue sliding hot and wet upon him. "You make me so hungry, Sweets. I want to lose myself in you, drink you in. Want to make you come, make you feel good."

*You do.* He nearly said the words out loud, cutting them off just in time. He arched his body as hard as he could, telling Bast without the words.

"I love you." The whisper rang loud in his ears, filling him with warmth, even as Bast's teeth slipped into him, suffusing him with pleasure.

Determined to preserve his silence for Bast, even as he came, Trick bit his lip, the taste of his own blood strong in his mouth. This was what Bast tasted when he fed. Between that thought and his lover's feeding, not even leather could stop his orgasm.

Bast suckled, moaning softly as wave after wave of sensation poured over him. Trick could hear everything -- every sigh and whisper and slide of tongue over his skin. The rest of the party was like a buzz at the back of his head, but each sound that Bast made, even the blink of his eyelids, lashes brushing against the sharp cheekbones, was audible.

Finally the bliss faded, Bast's mouth lifting from his skin, tongue sliding along blood-painted lips. "Delicious."

He reached out with his own tongue, tangling it with his lover's, another soft moan leaving him. The kiss lasted for long moments, Bast's hands curling in his hair. Sweet and lingering, Trick felt his energy levels rise as Bast loved him, feeding him with care and focus.

"I love you," he whispered, barely giving the words air.

"I know, Trick. Chosen." Bast's fingers brushed against his wrists, freeing him. Strong hands massaged the cramps from his shoulders, easing his arms to his sides.

He flexed his muscles and shifted, murmuring happily.

"Beautiful Trick." Bast nuzzled against him again, sigh brushing warm upon his skin.

He brought his arms up, holding Bast close. Chuckling, he ran his hand over the silk of Bast's shirt. "You aren't even naked," he murmured.

"You were too much to resist, Sweets." Bast undulated against him. "Let me get the leg cuffs off you and then you can molest me back... unless you and Rose have other plans?"

"I have no idea what the fuck Rose has planned, but I was a good boy for her all evening -- now, I want my reward." He leaned up and took a long kiss from Bast. "I want you."

"Yes." Bast tasted sweet, bright, full of a raw need laced through with energy.

Then the heat faded, his lover pulling away to kneel between his legs, unfastening his ankles. Trick got a lovely view of curved back and leather-covered ass. He reached down to caress the enticing buttocks, thumb sliding along Bast's crease, pressing the leather seam against skin.

Bast gasped, thighs parting. "Hold on, Sweets. You're

going to distract me."

Trick's laugh was husky and aroused and his hand slid down to cup Bast's balls from behind. "That's kind of the point."

Bast rocked against him, fingers frantic on his ankles. It took the vampire a moment, but eventually he was free, his lover's slender body writhing against his hand.

"Your hands feel good on my feet. I don't think you've ever fed from my ankles, baby-boy." A soft shudder went through him and he brought his other hand up to caress Bast's ass as he continued to fondle his lover's leather encased balls and cock.

"Oh, that's because, if I'm on my knees, I'm not usually going for your ankles."

That made him moan, his cock jerking, his hand tightening around Bast's genitals. A harsh groan sounded and Bast leaned forward to lick his ankles with a hot tongue, ass pushing up. Sharp nips caught his skin, Bast's tongue immediately soothing.

"Fuck, yeah..." He pushed himself up into a sitting position, leaning against Bast's back as he fondled his lover's ass and cock. He rubbed his cheek against the soft silk shirt. "Feel's good, baby-boy."

"You do." Bast's mouth moved over his feet, dozens of little sparks shooting through his body as he was tasted.

He groaned and hissed, the leather binding his own genitals keeping him from coming from the tiny bites, but if Bast took a real bite... He pushed his fingers against Bast's opening, pressing the leather as far as it would give, while his other hand stroked, hard and fast. "Do it."

"Yes." The strike was sharp and sweet, teeth sinking into him, overwhelming pleasure filling him immediately.

He sobbed, teeth biting into Bast's back through his

shirt as the shudders dragged pleasure through him. His orgasm felt long and slow and languid and incredible. He could feel his pleasure building and building in his balls and finally exploding from him in small spurts of heat.

Bast was whimpering against his flesh, body rocking harshly against him. "Sweets..."

He fumbled for a moment with Bast's zipper and then forced his fingers to function properly, pulling it down quickly but carefully. Bast's cock was hot and hard and so right in his hand and he stroked it, thumb sliding over the tip.

"Yeah, Sweets. Trick!" Wet heat splashed over his hand, Bast sobbing upon his skin.

Nuzzling through the silk shirt, Trick kept his hand moving, sliding slowly over Bast's cock, drawing out more shudders and shivery aftershocks. "Love you." He mouthed the words against Bast's back.

"Mmm. My Sweets." Bast nuzzled his legs, a low purr vibrating through his lover's body.

"Wow, who'd have thought foot sucking would be erotic." The shrill voice brought where they were screaming back to Trick's conscious -- he'd managed to block out their spectators, wrapping himself in the sensations that were Bast.

"Yeah, great show, Rose!"

Bast rolled until he was upright, purr darkening into something closer to a growl.

Trick rubbed his back. "We agreed to this, baby-boy. Next time we'll make her tell us up front what she's up to."

Bast leaned back against him, eyes closing. "Yeah. Yeah, you're right, Sweets."

"But now that we've given her friends their show...

take me home?"

"Yes. Rose, hand over Trick's clothes. We've got plans." Bast's voice held an edge of command, razor sharp.

Trick knew his thanks showed in his eyes.

His clothes materialized almost immediately and before anyone could comment, they were headed for the door, Bast giving Bael and Rose both a quick hug. Trick gave them each a perfunctory peck, not quite feeling in the mood for hugging them; he still felt strangely vulnerable and exposed.

"Come on, lover. Let's grab some good coffee and head home." Bast took his hand and headed again for the door.

He squeezed Bast's hand and let his lover lead him through the throngs of people, meeting eyes defiantly. He loved Bast, they were beautiful together; he had nothing to be ashamed of.

Bast turned as they reached the door, sliding into his arms, hands burying themselves in his hair as their lips met, Bast hot and loving against him. "I love you." The words weren't loud, but they were audible and proud and sincere.

A sweet shudder went through him at the public declaration and he whimpered into Bast's mouth, arms tightening around his lover. He suddenly had the feeling that Rose had seen far more than she'd bargained for.

Another soft, slow kiss and Bast backed away. "Home, Sweets."

He nodded and took Bast's hand again, striding confidently from the room.

# Chapter Twenty One

Rose had asked him how hungry he'd seen Bast. It made Trick think of that time they'd tried to go a month without Bast feeding off him; it made him think of the time he'd gone to his mother's wedding and had been gone a week; it made him think of the time Bast has been so wrapped up in a project, Trick had barely existed. None of them had been very much fun.

And then Rose had suggested a scenario to him and he'd come in his pants just thinking about it.

She and Bael were coming over at nine. He glanced at the clock -- that gave him a half hour to get Bast into position.

The vampire was just coming out of the shower, wiping his hair with a towel, otherwise quite naked.

"You look good enough to eat, baby-boy."

"Mm, Sweets. That's my line." Bast sauntered up to

him, nuzzling gently, towel still moving over the dark violet hair. "You smell good." Warm, damp lips moved over his throat, licking and lapping and tasting lazily.

He gasped, tilting his head back to give Bast better access to his neck. It was all he could do to step back before anything happened; Bast would feed on him tonight, but it would be better if he had to wait for it, if he was desperate for it: if they were both desperate for it. "I was thinking... maybe we could play a little game?"

"Sure, Sweets. Anything you want." Bast stretched, graceful and sleek beneath the blue lights. "I'm all yours. What's your pleasure?"

"Oh man, there're so many possibilities..." He tilted his head to the side and narrowed his eyes, hoping he looked like he was considering all those possibilities. "Oh, I know! Wait here, I'll be right back."

He gave Bast a quick kiss and then hurried to the bathroom and the box of toys they kept in the cabinet under the sink. He picked up the rope and elaborate cock ring he'd put aside early and then rummage a bit to make it look good. Going back out, he waved the rope and cock ring triumphantly.

Bast had moved over to the bed, a pair of thin pants laid out beside him. He grinned at Trick, one eyebrow arching skyward. "Oh, you want to *play*. Where should we put you, Sweets? The bed or the divan?"

He sauntered casually up to Bast. "Actually... I was thinking you'd look good in leather and rope."

"Me?" That eyebrow climbed even higher. "You are in a good mood tonight, Sweets. Okay, I'm game. Where do want me?"

"Hmm..." again he pretended to consider, looking from the bed to the divan and back again. "We just changed the sheets on the bed – let's do the divan. I'll put this on you on the bed though -- more comfortable for you to lie back on while I figure out which bit wraps around what."

Bast leaned forward, giving Trick a slow, burning kiss before settling back on the bed with a purr. "You're a bright boy. You can figure it out." Dark eyes glittered at him and Bast winked. "I have faith in you."

His chuckle was a little shaky, his eyes hot in his head as he watched Bast shift on the bed. He knelt next to the vampire and ran his hand up along soft as silk inner thighs. "I love you, Bast." He spoke the words quietly, gaze rising to meet Bast's eyes.

"I love you, too." Bast smiled, reached up and stroked his cheek. "Always."

He nuzzled against Bast's hand for a moment and then placed a quick kiss on the cool palm and another on the tip of Bast's cock. "Well at least I don't have to worry about getting you up first."

"No." Bast chuckled, hips pressing up slightly. "That's not a problem we have, as a rule, Sweets."

Trick grinned and swiped his tongue across the tip of Bast's cock. "Fuck, you taste good."

He paid close attention as he carefully looped the leather around Bast's balls, making sure they were clear of the leather and that he hadn't caught any skin. Satisfied, he tightened the leather and then circled it around the base of Bast's erection, snapping it closed. His fingers were gentle as they slid over the constricted flesh. "Is that all right?"

Bast moaned softly as he nodded, shifting beneath his touch. His lover's skin glowed against the maroon velvet, only the black leather breaking the smooth pale line. "Oh,

Sweets. I want you already."

"Yeah -- I know the feeling." Trick bent and placed a last, softly sucking kiss against the tip of Bast's cock and then scooped the vampire up into his arms, carrying him over to the divan.

Bast wrapped his arms around Trick's neck, face buried in his throat, nipping lightly -- little questioning bites that both threatened and promised more. A low purring filled the air, vibrating against his skin.

Trick shuddered and nearly tripped over his own feet, but he managed to get Bast to the divan without mishap. "You're being very bad, baby-boy," he whispered as he put his lover down behind the couch so he could bend Bast over it.

"Bad?" Bast's voice was silky and hot. "I thought I was being good, Sweets."

"Too good, and that's bad -- no feeding before I get you tied up."

"But Sweets, love... I'm hungry."

He shuddered and when he spoke his voice was thick with his own need. "Imagine how much better it'll be when you're even hungrier."

Bast's eyes flashed at him, golden and glowing. "Tie me now, Sweets, before I truly am bad."

"Fucking shit." He grabbed Bast's hands and looped the rope around them before bending his lover over the back of the divan and tying the rope to one of the legs. He then spread the lean legs and tied each one down. Leaning his cheek against Bast's thigh, he rubbed and then raised his head to lick at his lover's crease. "Do you have any idea how hard that was? Fuck, baby-boy, I wanted to let you feed so bad..."

"Why wait, sweet love?" Bast's body rocked, his

voice temptation itself. “I want you, Trick. Want to sink my teeth into your throat, into your cock.”

“Oh, fuck, yes!” Trick figured it was a pretty good thing he was behind Bast or the game would be all over. As it was he had to fight the urge to throw himself over the divan and shove his cock into Bast’s mouth. Instead he plunged his own tongue into Bast’s opening, his hand rubbing at his own cock through his jeans, whimpering.

If Rose and Bael didn’t show up soon he was going to forget why he was supposed to be waiting.

Bast growled low. “Oh, fuck. Trick. Your tongue... so hot, Sweets.”

The elevator began its noisy whine and grating as the echoes of Bast’s words faded. “Oh fuck. Whoever it is, Sweets, tell ‘em we’re busy. Tell ‘em we’re dead. Tell ‘em we’ll kill them. Whatever. Just make them go.”

He placed a kiss on one ass cheek and a bite on the other and then stood. “That would be kind of rude, baby-boy, especially as they were invited.”

Bast’s head lifted, confused, dark eyes searching for him. “Invited? Trick?”

He went back and gently stroked Bast’s cheek. “Just Rose and Bael.” Bending, he kissed each of Bast’s eyelids and then whispered. “A little fun to make you scream, baby-boy.”

Bast relaxed, eyes rolling as he grinned. “I’m going to kick Rose’s ass for this.”

Trick relaxed as Bast did and he made sure to trail his hand along his lover’s ass before he headed for the elevator. “I think the idea is that she gets to kick yours first.”

Bast groaned as Trick lifted the elevator grate, Rose and Bael waiting with expectant grins. Both in black, both bald as newborns -- beyond the color of their skin, they looked like mirror images of each other.

Rose's eyebrow arched at the noise and her smile widened as she looked past Trick into the room. "Mmm... there's a sight to warm a girl's heart. Good job, sugar."

Trick laughed. "It wasn't easy and I don't think he was even trying all that hard." He took their hands in his own and pulled them in. "Come on, let's get this party started."

Bael chuckled, wrapped Trick in a warm hug as Rose moved into the room to stroke her hand over Bast's ass. "Oh, Trick, we're going to have such fun. Rose and I have been excited all evening."

"You and Rose are always excited," he teased, letting his tongue slide along the shell of Bael's ear.

"Mmm... you have a point." Bael moaned, hand sliding to cup Trick's cock. "You seem to be excited yourself."

"I told you it wasn't easy." Trick began to rock into the hand that held him, groaning against Bael's lips.

"Come on, boys, bring the action over where our bad little boy here can see and smell and hear it. And take your clothes off so we can all enjoy the view." Her words were followed by a sharp crack and she grinned from her place behind Bast, holding up a small wooden paddle.

A single red mark was quickly fading on Bast's pale ass, returning with a vengeance as Rose swung the paddle again.

Bael walked Trick over to the divan so they were both in front of Bast's glittering eyes and continued rubbing Trick's cock with one hand while pulling at their clothes with the other.

As soon as they were both naked, Trick brought

their mouths together, humping against Bael's hand and grabbing Bael's ass. "You wanna fuck me?" he asked Bael.

Mmm... Yeah, Trick. Wanna fuck you nice and hard." Bael's hips pressed close, hard cock rubbing against his side. Bael looked over at Rose, who was rubbing Bast's ass slowly, paddle ready for another blow. "Where do you think, Rose honey? We want our boy to know what he's missing, right?"

"Oh yeah. Why don't you bend him over the coffee table -- Bast should be able to see every inch of your cock as it sinks into Trick that way. Isn't that right, Bast?" She let the paddle fly, the sound of wood on flesh loud.

Trick felt a shudder go through him at the sound, and he met Bast's gaze.

Bast's eyes were hot, hungry. "Want you, Sweets."

The paddle fell again, Bast's body rocking against its bonds, fluid and feral, hips canting up as if asking for the next blow.

Trick ran his hand along Bast's face. "I know, baby-boy, but you're going to have to wait until you can't stand it anymore."

He let his lips brush over Bast's, a soft, teasing kiss and slid the tip of his tongue against the side of that soft mouth and then turned and leaned over the coffee table.

He grabbed the other side of the table and spread his legs. Looking back over his shoulder, he grinned at Bael. "Show me what you've got."

Bael smiled back, fingers unwrapping a condom he'd fished from his discarded clothes. "You've seen what I've got, Trick lovely. It's just that usually your boy here's getting his own at the same time."

The dark-skinned man stepped close with a warm

chuckle and two slick fingers slid inside Trick's body, fucking him with sure, deep strokes. Bast's moan was audible over the arrhythmic slaps of the paddle and Rose's soft encouragements.

Trick spread his legs wider and pushed back against Bael's fingers. Everything seemed more intense like this, knowing that Bast was watching, that Bast wanted to be where Bael was, fucking him.

"Look at him, lover. So lovely, so hungry." Rose's voice was sultry, husky as she murmured to Bast. "Bael's gonna fuck him, slide into him so deep, lover."

Bast's choked moan was delicious, almost as good as the slow slide of Bael's cock into his body.

"Oh, yeah, Bael, fuck me slow and hard." He moaned softly as Bael's cock slid against his prostate, jolting pleasure along his spine.

Bael murmured nonsense words, hands sliding warm and soft over his back. The thrusts came slow and deep, each one filling him with one shot of pleasure after another. He rocked back against them, moaning, letting Bast hear his pleasure. The sounds of the paddle faded away as Bael fucked him, slow thrusts growing quicker and harder. Suddenly Rose's lips were on his, her callused fingers on his cheeks.

"Don't come, sugar. I want to watch you take your boy while his ass is on fire. Want you to feel how tight he is after the paddle."

"Oh, Fuck!" He brought their mouths together again, sucking hungrily on her tongue.

He stayed poised between the two sensations for as long as he could, the smoky, apple flavor of Rose's mouth filling his and Bael's cock driving him deeper and deeper into pleasure.

Finally he broke the kiss, gasping, reaching back with one hand to grab at Bael's thigh. "Stop, man. I'm gonna come."

Bael groaned softly and stilled, buried deep inside him. "Oh, Trick, man, I could fuck your sweet ass for days."

Rose chuckled and smiled up at Bael. "It's time for Trick to fuck our bad little boy. You'll just have to make do with my mouth, pretty boy. Oooh!" Her eyes lit up and she looked at Trick. "You think your boy can be trusted to use that mouth of his without biting?"

He chuckled as he realized what she had in mind. "It's me he wants -- I think you'll be safe enough." He didn't just think it, he knew it -- Bast wouldn't bite another soul as long as he lived to feed the vampire; that was his and his alone. Not that Bael and Rose needed to know that.

"Mmm... wonderful." She gave him another slow, deep kiss, hands sliding down his neck and over his shoulders. "You're so fun so play with, sugar. Love the feel of your skin."

Bast whimpered softly and she grinned. "Let me warm him up again and get settled. You're gonna love this."

Bael slid from his body, both of them groaning as he did. Trick wasn't too steady on his feet and he trailed his fingers over Bast's body as he made his way to the back of the divan, eager to watch Rose work Bast's ass.

Rose stripped quickly, rubbing against Bast's body before picking up the paddle. "No one moves under the paddle like your boy, Trick. He's responsive as fuck, hot and sensual. None of this 'oh, punish me' shit. Bast just rides the heat and the rush."

She began the oddly rhythmic blows again, turning Bast's ass from pink to a glowing red.

"Fuck, you're beautiful, baby-boy." He slid his hand along Bast's inner thigh, fingers brushing lightly over the bound sacs and shaft.

"Trick, Sweets!" Bast jerked into his hand, body convulsing at the touch. The normally cool skin was hot, burning against him.

Rose reached down and squeezed gently at the leather bonds holding Bast's balls captive. "No, lover. You don't get to come; you don't get to feed. You just get to feel."

Trick bit his lip, caught on the edge between enjoying watching Bast squirm and needing to give his lover what he needed -- what they both wanted. Only the fact that they would let Bast feed from him once the anticipation and hunger had been ratcheted up to the highest possible point allowed him to continue.

Blood slid into his mouth from where he was biting his lip and it made him moan, made his cock jerk; his blood was Bast's.

Rose's hand slid around his hip, pulling him close to the heat pouring off Bast. "Come on, sugar. He's ready for you."

She slid his cock against Bast's entrance, teasing them both. "Do you want him, lover? Want him inside you?"

"Yes, fuck. Yes. Now. Please, Sweets. Please."

"Fuck, yes." Trick pushed in without fanfare, without hesitation; he thrust into Bast, deep and hard, moaning at the tight heat that grasped at him. He didn't stop until his hips were pressed against Bast's burning hot ass. Bast cried out, pushing back toward Trick as much as the bonds would allow, rubbing his fiery skin against Trick.

Rose's chuckles filled the air as she moved before Bast, leaning in to brush the dark tousled hair away from his face and kiss him. "Want you to lick me, lover, thank me for making you so hot. 'kay?" Bast trembled, nodding and offering another kiss.

Bael stood behind Trick, nuzzling his shoulders, watching Rose and Bast.

Trick grabbed Bast's ass and squeezed the red flesh, moaning as Bast's body tightened around him. He began a slow rhythm, watching Rose and Bast as he fucked his lover. There was an energy flowing between them, like they were all connected together, sharing their heat; it all began with him and Bast and spread to the other two as they played together so often. There was just one link missing to close the circle.

"Bael... fuck me."

Bael's answer was a soft moan and the slide of heated flesh inside him, joining his rhythm, helping him to push deeper into Bast. They rocked together, deep moans mingling with soft sighs and pleas for more, harder, faster, please.

All his senses were engaged as the four of them fucked together, Bast their center, their focal point. Everything beyond the slap of skin, the scent of sex, the moans and whimpers of pleasure, the heat and pounding and naked flesh disappeared from his consciousness.

He had no idea how long they moved together, only that it was too long and it wasn't long enough and someone screamed and then he was coming, they were all coming, all of them except Bast, who writhed at their centre, bound and unsated.

Bast was moaning continuously, body still moving on Trick's cock. Rose moved, reaching in her bag and pulling out a plug, letting Bast see it. Bast's body tightened again, a desperate noise sounding.

Rose slicked it lightly and handed it to Trick with a

truly evil grin. "This'll keep him busy while we recover. It's a handy little gadget. Vibrates -- has a remote control and everything."

Bael slid out of Trick's body, whispering low. "Trust her, babe. When he breaks, it's like nothing you've ever seen."

He slid out of Bast with a sigh, nodding at Bael's words, even as he fought himself; it was killing him not to give Bast what he wanted -- what they both wanted, and it was getting harder to deny his lover by the second.

Trick pushed the plug in quickly and then took off, heading to the bathroom to clear his head.

Rose followed him in, hands moving to his shoulders. "What's up, sugar? You not having fun? We can stop anytime, pretty love. Anytime you want."

He leaned against the counter, letting her touch soothe him. "I didn't think it would be so hard to deny him, 'cause it's only for a bit, you know? It's not like he's going to die if he doesn't feed right now, but still." Trick shook his head and continued in a whisper. "I need to give it to him as much as he needs to take it, Rose. It's like a drug, knowing he's hungry, knowing I'm what he needs, offering myself, being taken."

Her hands continued to move, soft and easy. "It is a bit of a drug, I think. None of us got hooked like you. I mean, Bael was close, but I think he gives you something he couldn't give us."

A soft kiss landed on his shoulder. "Just remember, sugar, if he *needs*, those ropes are nothing. He vamps out and he could shrug out of them. He wants. He's hungry. But he's there because he wants to be. He knows it'll be good. Hell, this is *Bast* we're talking about -- the boy is seduction on legs. Let him try, let him talk and beg, baby. In the morning, when you're both sated and sore and snuggled together, you'll be flying."

"I know you're right, I just needed a few minutes to let it sink in." Just then Bast moaned loudly and Trick grinned at Rose. "Come on, he's putting on a show -- the least we could do is watch."

Rose giggled, eyes suddenly young and girlish, contrastingly oddly with her bald head. "God, yes. Besides, you don't want to leave Bael alone with him too long, Bast will convince him to untie the ropes. Bael doesn't top well, you know?"

He grinned, feeling suddenly much better about the whole thing, strong enough to see it through to the end, to push Bast until his lover broke and took what he needed by force.

Trick slid his arm around Rose's shoulder and headed them back out. "Unlike you, Rosie -- you're problem is you don't even know what a bottom is."

She butted his shoulder easily with her head. "Sure I do, sugar. That's the other guy."

They walked in just in time. Bael was kneeling in front of Bast, Bast talking to him soft and low, eyes glittering. Trick could see Bael's shudders from across the room.

"Oh, dear me, Rose, would you look at what we have here." He moved over to Bast and began to fondle his buttocks, fingers sliding down to bump at the plug inside Bast and then to slide over the bound and straining flesh beyond. "You're being a very bad boy. I think it's time to show you what happens to very bad boys."

Rose draped herself over Bael, grinning at Bast as he arched and cried out. "Were you trying to tempt our pretty Bael?" She nipped at Bael's ear. "You know better than to listen to our wicked, bad boy, pretty."

"Where's the remote control for this thing?" Trick asked as he again bumped the plug with his fingers. "I think Bael should be in charge of it -- he can keep Bast on the edge while I let you top me where Bast can see, Rose."

Both Bael and Bast groaned, the sounds floating in the air beneath Rose's laughter. "Sounds perfect, sugar."

Bast's voice broke through the laughter. "Trick... Sweets. Let me taste you first? Let me... oh, fuck..." His voice broke, as Rose found the remote and pushed a button.

Trick laughed, pushing away his need. He wandered over to Rose and took the remote from her, 'accidentally' adjusting one of the settings as he tossed it to Bael. "On the other side of us -- where he can't seduce you into changing the settings to what he wants." He turned his attention to Bast then, looking into eyes full of desperate hunger. "I'm all yours, Rose, how do you want me?"

"Kneeling in front of Bast, sugar. If he's a quiet little vampire, I'll let you come on his face when I'm done." Rose looked over at Bael with a grin. "You keep him off-balance and crazy and I'll fuck you into the floor when I'm done with Trick."

Bael groaned, one hand on the remote, one on his cock, pulling it steadily. "You're a wanton, horny bitch, Rose."

Trick grinned and knelt, facing Bast. His cock was hard again, his balls aching. "So what are you going to do with me, Rose?"

She pulled her bag over, kneeling behind Trick. "You're the type who can be driven mad with pleasure, sugar, not pain." Her body moved behind him, soft and warm as she rummaged. "The secret of topping is knowing what makes your lover fly."

Warm fingers teased at his nipples for a minute and then smooth-edged clamps were slipped on, little vibrating eggs attached to the ends. She tightened them slowly, making him moan.

"Things like this." She flipped a switch and they began to hum.

"Fuck!" He shuddered and he reached out, holding onto the edge of the divan to stay upright. His eyes met Bast's and he laughed. "And here I thought we were supposed to be torturing you," he said quietly.

Bast's head dipped, tongue stretching out to lick along his knuckle, dark eyes flashing gold. Then a button clicked and Bast's eyes closed, body shuddering.

Trick's chuckle was short lived as the eggs' vibrations became stronger. "Bael was right," he whispered, "you are a wanton, horny bitch, Rose."

Her hand cupped his balls, a powerful vibrating egg pressed firmly behind them. "Yes, sugar. I am. And you all love it."

She leaned up, sucking on Trick's throat, her teeth resting on his skin. It felt strange and wrong and suddenly he wasn't having fun anymore.

Bast's eyes went gold and the divan trembled and creaked. Trick heard a low snarl rip through the air. "Mine."

"Fuck, yeah," he agreed, head automatically tilting for Bast's bite, his eyes closing as small shudders moved through him. He whimpered, waiting for Bast to break and take him.

"You want him, lover?" Rose's voice was low, tight, an edge of nervousness within it. "But I have him."

Trick groaned as her teeth scraped over his skin. No.

No, he was Bast's. This wasn't hers.

A series of noises sounded -- a snarling-creaking-snapping growl that seemed to fill the air and suddenly he was flying, yanked from Rose's arms, somehow cradled in Bast's arms upon the bed.

Bast was growling, eyes bright in the shadows around the bed, face feral and wild. "Mine."

"Yes. Please." He arched up pushing against Bast, head back, legs opening, offering himself to Bast. Tremors moved through him as he waited. "Please."

"Mine." Trick was tumbled onto the mattress. Bast curled over him, incredibly strong hands pulling him onto burning hard flesh even as teeth pierced his throat.

He screamed and screamed and screamed, body jerking between the points of penetration. It felt like lightning striking, or exploding into a million pieces, or pleasure so extreme it was pain or pain so extreme it was pleasure. Bast was in him and on him and around him and their hearts were beating as one and Bast was in his blood and his blood was in Bast. Red exploded behind his eyes -- bright and shining like the sun just as it sets and then growing steadily darker until it was the color of wine and then the color of blood and then black darkness took him, wrapped him in velvet.

It was Rose's voice that woke him. "Trick, Trick sugar. Come on now. Come back to us."

He was wrapped in the comforter, the smell of orange juice sharp and clear. "Come on, now. Drink some juice, Trick. Open your eyes."

"Bast?" His voice was barely audible, low and rough. He slowly opened his eyes, blinking. "Where's Bast?"

"There you are." Rose's eyes were bright and she pressed the glass of juice to his lips. It tasted good, cold.

"Fuck, you two scared us."

He drank greedily and then pushed the glass away. "Scared you? Where's Bast?"

"Yeah, man." Bael sat down next to him. "You screamed like you were dying and we tried to pull Bast off you, but he wouldn't go and then... well, you've been out for a while. Rose and I were about to call an ambulance. Drink the juice up and we'll mix up something with iron in it. You're still pale as a sheet."

He struggled to get up, fought with them as worry shot through him. "Where the fuck is Bast?"

"Chill! Chill." Rose sighed. "We sent him off to take a walk for a few days, get his fucking head back on straight. He really lost it, you know? He's going to have to learn to control that possessive thing before he kills you."

"What the fuck are you talking about? You sent him away and he let you?" Trick fell back, against the sheets, his strength gone. "Trust me, you said. Wait until he loses it, you said -- well, he did and he took me and you were right; it was fucking amazing. Fucking shit!" He struggled to get up again. "What the hell is he supposed to do when the sun comes up -- I can't believe he let you send him away. Help me the fuck up!"

Rose pushed him down. "Bast is a big boy. He'll deal. You have to relax, sugar. Bast is coming back. You... fuck, Trick, you scared us. I mean, I've seen Bast vamped out, we all have, but this was different. He wouldn't let us near you, wouldn't let us touch you. We thought he was going to kill you."

Her voice was somber. "It stopped being sex when that whole 'mine' thing happened, sugar. That's not cool. That's not Bast."

He laughed, choking the sound off before it could become a sob. It hadn't been 'sex' for a very long time: not for him, not for Bast. How did she not know that – she'd seen them together often enough. "Get him back."

"Sugar..."

"I said get him back -- I need him. I'm not eating or drinking another thing until you go out there and find him." He swallowed and looked her straight in the eye. "And if you won't, I will."

Rose looked at Bael. "You know where he'd go, pretty?"

Bael nodded. "The bridge until dawn and then underground. You try his cell and I'll head up. Keep Trick here. He's in no shape to be outside."

"In the morning, when you're both sated and sore and snuggled together, you'll be flying. You remember saying that to me, Rose? I want that. You promised me that and then you sent him away." He closed his eyes, taking shallow breaths, body feeling light and unreal.

Trick couldn't shake the urgency, the need to have Bast wrapped around him. He'd passed out before when Bast had fed, when they'd been having wild, incredible sex and Bast had held off and then taken him, but Bast has always been there after, holding him, energizing him.

Bast had never fed from him and then let him go. It was wrong that he had gone this time.

"What did you say to him? I can't believe he left while I was still out -- what did you say to him?"

"Nothing. Just the truth." Rose stood and began to pace. "Damn. Damn. It's one thing to play with a bunch of us, you know? One thing for it to be sex and fun. This though... this need thing. It's wrong, sugar, wrong for him to do this to you. He's fucking with your brain, with your insides."

She stopped, looking across the room at him. "We told him we'd call the cops if he didn't give it a few days. Bast needs to stay low; can you imagine what a morning in an exercise yard would do for him? Bael had the phone; I've got blood soaked sheets from where we tried to pull him off. He decided to take a walk. As least let your head clear before he comes back."

"It's not about the sex, Rose. It hasn't been about the sex for a long time, not since I've known what he was." He pushed himself up onto his elbows. "The phone, Rose -- call his cell now. Get him here before the sun comes up. You don't understand what's between us, but he isn't doing anything to me. I'm the one who started it. I'm the one who asked him not to feed from anyone but me. I'm the one who can't go much more than a week without it. It isn't him, okay? It's me. It's me. Me."

Rose shook her head, but walked across the room and picked up the phone. A few short moments, some harshly whispered words and she slammed down the phone. Rose turned toward him, tears in her eyes. "I'm going. I'm sorry, Trick. I should've listened to him. He's in a fury. Said to tell you he'd be home in a second."

Relief shot through him, replacing the fear and worry and anger, the last of his energy going with those emotions, leaving him exhausted and shaking. He thought maybe he was crying, but he really didn't know and didn't care. Bast would be there soon, holding him and then he'd be okay. "Thank you, Rose."

Trick floated there on the bed, the elevator working impossibly long to take Rose up. Suddenly, the mattress dipped and cool hands were moving over his body, Bast's voice warm in his ear. "Oh, Sweets, you okay, love? You doing alright?"

He gasped and searched blindly, arms wrapping around Bast's neck. He didn't think he'd ever let go. "You weren't here."

"Fucking idiots, thought I'd hurt you." Bast wrapped them together in the blankets, sweet kisses pouring over his face. "They wigged out and were gonna call the cops, Sweets. I'd be fucked in jail, you know?" Bast nuzzled him gently. "Knew you'd wake up in a few and give them what for, so I just paced around and waited."

He nodded and just held on, the shakes slowly subsiding.

Bast crooned and stroked, keeping him close. "Love you, Sweets. Except for the very end, it was very fun, love. You made me wild."

He grinned against Bast's skin. "Until I woke up it was a pretty fucking great ride. When Rose put her teeth on me..." a soft shudder went through him, "I knew you wouldn't let her do that, I knew if she didn't back down you'd take me from her. Shit, that flying thing --what the fuck was that? Amazing."

Bast chuckled. "More like a jump, Sweets. Some of the shit that happens when we go feral -- it's intense. I saw her teeth against you and just saw red." Bast's voice had dropped, grown husky again. "My Sweets."

"Yours." He felt heavy, exhaustion demanding its payment. "Saw red, too. 'Fore I passed out. Like I was our blood or something."

"You are, love. You are." Bast's lips brushed across his eyelids.

Trick sighed; he wasn't going to be awake very much longer. "I love you."

"Sleep, Sweets." Bast kissed him one last time.

"You'll be here when I wake up?"

"Where else would I be, love? This is where I belong."

"I know." He nuzzled into Bast and let himself go, the slow thump of his lover's heart beneath his ear following him into sleep.

# Chapter Twenty Two

Bast was stretching, water pouring over him, steam filling the air. Trick was sleeping, had been resting, recovering for the last few days. His lover would have been fine, wouldn't have been so exhausted had Rose and Bael let them stay together, let him bring Trick down, let him ease Trick back into his own body.

He knew they meant well, knew they didn't understand -- fuck, he wasn't quite sure he understood, just knew he needed his Chosen deep within, but Trick was the one who paid for it.

He grabbed the soap, began to stroke it along his body, sighing at the sweet slide of his hands against his skin.

"Now, isn't that a sight made to make a man hard?" Trick drawled the words lazily and Bast looked up to find his Sweets leaning against the back wall, watching him with avid eyes. He turned with a grin, posing and preening for Trick's eyes, hand dropping to lather the black curls at his groin.

Trick made a noise that was a cross between a moan and a whimper and he fell onto his knees, licking at the tip of Bast's cock. Blue eyes gazed up at him, almost black with need. "Rinse the soap off."

He nodded, turning toward the spray, rinsing the bitter suds away without a word, before turning back to his lover. "All clean."

Trick's mouth closed over his cock, drawing him in deep, sucking strongly. Square hands cupped his ass, pulling him in deeper.

"Oh, Sweets, love!" So good, mind-numbingly good -- he loved sucking Trick, loved the feel and flavor of the hard cock in his lips. Sometimes he forgot -- by all the little gods, how could he forget? -- how good it felt to have Trick's mouth on him.

Trick let the edges of his teeth scrape along Bast's cock. When he looked down at his Sweets the blue eyes were gazing up at him, full of mischief and love.

"Tease." His voice was hunger and laughter and sweet pleasure.

The mischief in Trick's eyes grew deeper and the next scrape of teeth brought soft flashes of pain with it and then Trick began to suck in earnest. The humming began a moment later, sending vibrations all along his cock. He arched, his moan loud as it bounced along the marble tiles. Sweet pleasure rushed through him, wave after wave of sensation pulled out by Trick's mouth. His Sweets' fingers danced along is cleft, teasing.

"Oh, yes..." He looked down into Trick's eyes. "Fuck me, love? I want to feel you inside me."

Need flared in the blue depths and then Trick was releasing him with a soft kiss to the tip of his cock. His Sweets stood, and pressed against him. "Up against the wall, baby-boy? With the water falling down around us?"

"Yes." He wrapped his arms around Trick's neck, bringing their mouths together in a long, slow kiss.

Trick reached over for the soap and handed it to him. "Lather me up and then turn around and put your hands on the tiles."

With an anticipatory shiver, Bast built up a large lather, teasing them both by starting at Trick's shoulders and slowly moving down, hands feeling each muscle, each plane and dip and curve.

"And you called me a tease." Trick's voice was thick.

"Yes, my tease." He let his hand slip down onto Trick's cock, slicking it with quick, firm strokes. Trick's eyes half-closed, his moan soft, almost a whimper. "My sweet, delicious, fucking lovely tease." Bast leaned forward, nipping softly below Trick's ear.

"Be careful, baby-boy. You start biting now and it'll all be over before you get fucked."

"No, no. Fuck me first, Sweets. Please." He whispered softly. "Fuck me and then we'll go to bed and do it again and *then* I'll feed. I want you."

"Oh yeah, I like the sound of that. Turn around."

Bast nodded, humming happily as he turned, stretching up along the wall, spreading his legs in invitation.

"Yeah... just like that." Trick's fingers found him first, two sliding into him, slick with soap and then sliding out again to be replaced by the hard heat of his lover's' cock.

Bast arched and pressed back, pleasure and hunger filling him along with Trick's flesh. "Good."

"Yes." Trick slid his hands from Bast's shoulders, up along his arms until they rested overtop of his hands, sliding their fingers together. Trick started with long, slow strokes that let him feel every inch of that thick cock. Bast held on to Trick's hands, letting his head fall backward as Trick moved within him. He was making soft, hungry noises that joined with the falling water.

Trick's mouth slid over his shoulder, warm tongue lapping at the water on his skin. "So fucking sexy." The words were whispered against him.

"You make me hungry. Make me hot." Bast undulated on Trick's cock, eyes closed so he could feel everything -- every motion, every sweet slow press of flesh within him, every touch of tongue.

Whimpering, Trick's hips thrust faster, deeper. One arm came down to wrap around his waist, holding him in place as Trick moved into him.

"Yes." Bast pressed back against him, encouraging the thrusts. "Love when you fuck me, Sweets."

The water pounded down on them, wet and hot, but not as hot as Trick's cock stroking into him.

His orgasm started low in his belly, curling up his spine and down his thighs and all through his balls before pumping his pleasure through his cock. He didn't cry out, just let the sweet sensations move through him, pulsing and warm. Trick groaned as he tightened around the hard cock. Several more thrusts and then Trick was calling out, his name, muffled against his shoulder as warmth filled him.

"Love you. So good, Trick.." Warm and sated and wet and steam and Trick and he was going to have to install a padded mattress in here...

"Oh, baby-boy, I love you, too." Trick nuzzled below

his ear and they both sighed as Trick's cock slid from Bast's body.

It was Trick who led him from the shower, wrapping a towel around his body and drying him off before leading him back to bed.

Bast curled up on the mattress, snuggling close, hands moving to trace patterns on Trick's skin. "You feeling better, Sweets?"

"Yeah." Trick moved into his touches, nuzzling into his neck and almost purring.

Without warning, the elevator began to creak and groan. Trick raised his head, frowning. "You expecting anyone?"

Bast frowned. "No. No, I'm not."

Only a few people had the elevator key -- Rose and Bear, Bael. He stood and pulled on a pair of silky pants, tossing Trick his jeans.

Trick sighed and pulled the jeans on, grabbing a t-shirt out of the drawer and his black leather jacket from over the back of a chair and striking what Bast privately called his defensive pose. "You know it's Rose. Maybe she dragged Bear and Bael with her -- but you know she's the only one of the three with the balls to show up here unannounced, especially after..."

Bast nodded as the elevator doors opened. Bael and Bear stood on either side of Rose, their attitude defensive. He looked over at Trick with a grin. "The troops are here to rescue you, Sweets. If they come after me with crosses and stakes, I vote we go dancing."

Trick didn't even try to grin back, all his attention on the three stepping into the apartment. "What do you want?"

Rose's face was stiff, cool. "We wanted to see if you

were okay, sugar."

Bast frowned. "I didn't hurt him, mijita. Come now, I wouldn't hurt him. Have I *ever* hurt any of you?"

"I was fine until you interfered," Trick added vehemently.

Bear looked over at Trick, rumbling unhappily. "They said you screamed, sugar. They said Bast wouldn't let you go."

"Of course I screamed -- it was the best fucking thing I'd ever felt. I scream in bed -- you guys know this. And Bast knew what he was doing -- I trust him. And I thought you did, too."

Bast walked up to Rose. "I love him, mijita. I wouldn't hurt him. I *won't* hurt him."

Rose frowned. "This isn't about you, Bast. It's about Trick."

"Yeah, well, I love Bast, too, and I won't hurt him, either." Trick had crossed his arms over his chest and hadn't come over to where they were all standing.

Bast couldn't decide if he was more hurt that they thought he would harm Trick, amused by their posturing, or unnerved by the scent of danger in the air.

"What did you guys want? To see that Trick was okay? He's right here. He's fine. Next time, give a guy a ring and I'll even put a shirt on for you."

"We've talked about this before," Bael said softly. "You said you had everything in hand, it doesn't look like everything's in hand, lover. It looks like the two of you are playing some dangerous, wigged-out game."

A soft, angry noise came from behind him, but Trick remained otherwise silent.

"Bael." The censure, the suggestion, the thinly veiled distrust -- those did hurt, sliced deep and wide. Bael was his friend, had been his friend longer than anyone since Bryce.

"Maybe it's the intensity between you two, Bast. You've never moved someone in, made them so much of your life." Bear's voice sounded sad, tired. "You've always been so free, Bast."

"So you guys are upset that he's happy?" Trick headed slowly toward them, slinking in that predatory way that had first attracted Bast to him. "Or is it really that you're upset he's happy without you?"

Rose shook her head. "No, sugar, all we're saying is maybe there's a *reason* Bast is so free and easy. Maybe his kind shouldn't get emotionally involved. Maybe he's making you sick, making you *his*."

"Oh, for fuck's sake!" Bast looked at Bear, who seemed to be the only one of the three who would really look back at him. "Have I ever hurt you, Bear? Ever hurt *anyone* in all the time you've known me? I fucking love Trick -- more than I've ever loved anyone in almost seven hundred years. Do you really think I'd hurt him?"

Trick's arms circled him from behind, cool, trembling fingers sliding over his stomach, petting. Trick's head rested against his shoulder. "More than anyone, baby-boy?" Trick's whisper was barely audible, for his ears only.

His Sweets' voice rose as he addressed the trio in front of them. "I know better than any of you what an abusive relationship looks like. I got up close and personal demonstrations. I'm not sick. Bast isn't making me anything."

"Cool. Prove it." Bael's voice was clipped, odd and unfamiliar in Bast's ears. "Come with us, Trick. Spend a few days in the sun. Give your neck a break. See a doctor and let him check your blood, just to make sure. A physical, you know?"

Bast forced himself not to stiffen in protest, but he couldn't stop his stomach muscles from clenching beneath Trick's fingers, couldn't stop his breath from catching.

Trick laughed, actual humor in the sound. "You think he's turning me into a vampire?"

"We didn't say that, sugar." Rose took a step forward, Bast instinctively pressing back against Trick. "We just think a doctor should check you out. Anemia, you know?"

"I take plenty of iron pills, eat lots of red meat. Besides, I can't afford a doctor."

Trick's arms had tightened around him, wrists still looped casually at his waist. Pressed as close as he was, Bast could feel the tension in Trick's body, like his Sweets could also feel the warnings in the air.

"Bast can. Hell, I saw the paperwork after Bast left before. You own all this. He made sure you had a place." Bael moved in close and Bast had to force himself not to snap out, protect his family from the predators.

He could feel the beast, feel the urges that screamed that encroachers had invaded the home territory, that his family, his mate, his Chosen was being threatened. Bast lost track of the conversation for a moment, focusing on his humanity, his civilized nature.

Trick was speaking, he could hear the angry rumble against his back. "-that he has to check for stuff because I'm fucking a vampire? He'll throw me in the mental ward and throw away the fucking key. You want me to go out and stand in the sun, prove I can do it -- fine, I'll do that, but you know what? Not until I get some kind of guarantee from the three of you that you aren't going to take the opportunity to kidnap me and drag me off somewhere, 'cause I have to tell you that this doesn't feel like a concerned little visit, this feels like you're up to something, something you know Bast and me aren't gonna like."

"It's time for you three to go. Leave the elevator keys." Bast stroked Trick's hand, soothing them both. He felt ill, filled with a mixture of sorrow and anger and fear. "This is our home and you were not invited here today. I am not hurting him. I have not hurt him. I have not hurt you."

He could feel Trick, stiff and straight behind him, could well imagine the defiant, angry look on his Sweets' face, he'd had it directed at himself a time or two, though not in a long while.

"Not hurt him? Fuck, Bast! You nearly *killed* him!" Rose's dark eyes were flashing, her face flushed and furious. "I saw him after -- he was as pale as you are, shaky, couldn't find his ass with both hands. You owe us an explanation, Bast. Why did you go nuts? Why did you damn near suck him dry? How do we know you won't hurt him again?"

"I'd have been fine if you hadn't interfered!"

Bast squeezed Trick's hand, mind whirling. He didn't owe them anything, hadn't hurt anyone.

"Oh, really? What? Bast bites you and sucks you dry and you don't mind?" Bael laughed. "Fuck man, he's got you seriously hooked."

"He didn't suck me dry and if you had let him finish, he would have made sure I was fine before he was done." Trick sounded angrier than Bast could ever remember his lover being, even when they'd broken up.

"How, Trick? Come on, *think* about it. How does he

do it? Why does he only feed on you now? He fucking flew across the room, snarling and wrapped around you like some kind of monster, like an animal." Rose shook her head. "It's not a game anymore, Trick. He's *feeding* off you, like he needs you and you're all into it! It's got to stop."

"Fuck you, Rose. You haven't a clue what you're talking about." Trick stepped around Bast to tower over Rose, anger radiating from him. "I asked him not to feed off anyone but me. I'm the one who set up the regular delivery of blood from the bank."

Trick laughed, the sound hard and humorless. "He almost never asks. He doesn't have to, he knows I'll offer when I want him to feed and he's content to live off the bagged blood in between." Not that he'd had to use the bagged blood in a long, long time. It was just him and Trick now. "You think he's possessive of me? I'm the possessive one, Rose. He's mine, his feeding is mine and I'm not here because he's forcing me or tricking me or for any reason other than it is exactly where I want to be and I resent you coming in here and throwing around accusations about stuff that you have no idea about.

"We let you into our fucking home, into our bedroom and our bodies. And now that isn't' enough for you, now you want this, too? Well you can't have it -- it's mine and his and not any of your business."

Bast moved forward, hands sliding over Trick's back. "Trick's right. You're our friends, but this is ours, not open for discussion or complaint or your viewing pleasure. I don't have to justify this to you, Rose. You're not involved. None of you are."

"Bast. Babe. This is what we're talking about." Bael's eyes were damp, face unhappy. "You never used to keep us out, babe. Never used to pick favorites. Never used to scare us."

"Fucking shit, I was right the first time. You are jealous."

Rose shook her head at Trick. "We're concerned. We all had a good thing and it's changed, sugar. What you two have is different, scary. Maybe wrong, sugar. We don't want you hurt, Trick."

"I haven't hurt him." Bast sighed, burying his face against Trick's back. "I haven't hurt any of you."

"What's wrong is you coming here with your accusations. Bast has been nothing but good to all of you and you repay him by hurting him like this." One of Trick's hands covered his as it rested on his Chosen's shoulder. "What's it going to take to get the three of you out of here and leaving this alone?"

"Come with us, Trick. Spend a few days in the sun, take a few days off, a few days without Bast and just think about this. That's all we're asking." Rose's voice was beginning to grate against Bast's nerves. "We can go to the movies, play, just hang out. After a few days, you still feel the same way, you can come back and we'll drop it."

Trick was shaking his head. "No. I'm not leaving him. I already left him once and we were both miserable. Bael knows how awful that time was. I knew what I was getting into when I came back to him."

"I think it's not me and Trick that need a few days off." Bast looked up and met Rose's eyes. He was done. He was sad and upset and ready for these people to leave his family alone. "I think you should go. For a few days, a few weeks, whatever. But it's time for you to go."

She crossed her arms, face set, the very epitome of

stubborn. "I told the boys when we got on this elevator we weren't going unless we had Trick with us or were satisfied with the answer you gave us. Well I can't speak for the boys, but *I* am not satisfied."

Bear remained quiet, but Bael was shaking his head. "I'm still worried, too. I don't like what I've seen. It's going to hurt both of you in the end."

He couldn't believe this. Bast just stood, silent and still, caught between fury and pain and utter disbelief. These people had come to *take* his lover, thought he would hurt Trick -- his Sweets, his lifeblood, his mate, his *Chosen*?

Bast would stand burning beneath the noonday sun, let himself be whipped with wooden switches, would pour his own blood out before doing harm to Trick.

Trick was shaking his head again. "I still think the lot of you are jealous. He was your friend first, your toy; you got to play and flirt with danger and *feel* it when he bit you, come when the kiss of his teeth sent you flying and then I show up and suddenly you don't get that anymore, suddenly your plaything is gone.

"Oh, he'll still let you fuck him, let you beat him and play him and be with him, but you've lost that thing that made doing it with Bast special and so you're determined to take it away from me, too.

"You've got yourselves convinced that you're down here because you're worried about me -- but the truth is that you want what I've got. Well, you can't have it -- Bast doesn't love you, not like that. Now I suggest that you get the fuck out of here before he decides that he doesn't even like you anymore."

It was Bear that spoke up into the resulting silence, voice soft and steady. "We need to go, Rose. Trick's where he wants to be and I've never seen Bast hurt anyone. We should go."

"But..." Rose's voice was sheer fury.

"Now, Rosie." The big hand fell on her shoulder. "Now."

"Listen to him, Rose, while there's still a chance you can come back after we've all calmed down. Go before one of us says something we can never get over." Trick sounded like he wasn't entirely sure that hadn't already happened.

Rose looked like she was about to argue when Bear gently and quietly handed Bast a key and turned Rose toward the elevator. "Give him the key, Bael. We're leaving."

Trick held out his hand and Bael deposited his key in it with a show of reluctance. "Be safe."

Bast turned and walked to the bed, sitting on the edge and closing his eyes. The elevator rumbled and squeaked as it took them up and away. Sorrow and something too close to loss filled him and he let them wash through, leaving him feeling raw and empty.

Trick's hands slid over his shoulders and pulled him against the now-naked abdomen, his Sweets caressing his back, his neck, fingers sliding gently through his hair. "I'm sorry, baby-boy."

"Not your fault." He buried his face in the soft skin, letting his hot tears fall silently.

Trick pushed him back onto the bed, following him down and licking away his tears. Nimble fingers undid the button and zipper on his pants, working them off. Bast just relaxed, letting Trick care for him, letting Trick touch him. Letting Trick love him.

After pulling off his pants Trick moved him into the

middle of the bed, hands and lips and tongue moving over him with warm, gentle caresses. He was warm and floating, not thinking about anything but his lover and how right and sweet and good it felt between them.

Trick spread his legs, lifted them so his ankles rested on the warm shoulders and then he was entered. One long, firm thrust after another filled him, sending him flying. Trick leaned forward, bending him almost double, the new angle finding the hard cock stroking against his prostate with every thrust. Trick's lips found one of his nipples, tugging on it.

"Oh, my Trick. My sweet love. Yes, please." He was babbling, soft, gentle words of love and encouragement and sheer fucking pleasure. "I need you, Trick. Want you. Need you so."

"I love you, Bast." The words were soft against his skin.

One of Trick's hands slid around his head, pulling him down until his face was pressed against Trick's neck. "Feed, baby-boy. Take what you need."

"My love." He whispered the words against Trick's skin before he bit down, drinking deeply, letting the sweet rush of Trick inside him soothe him.

Trick's scream was more of a sob, cock shoving deep, seed filling him even as Trick's blood did. Bast came with a cry, suckling softly, tears pouring down his face as he relaxed. He slowly closed the wound, sucking and licking at Trick's skin.

Trick shifted, gently sliding from his body, moving his legs down, fingers massaging his thighs. Lips closed over his, the kiss deep, but so soft, Trick's tongue like a butterfly in his mouth. Then Trick was leaning over him, looking down at him and stroking his cheek, fingers wiping away tears. "I love you."

"I love you. I didn't mean to hurt them, Trick. I don't understand." He tried to smile, tried for light and easy-going. "You'd think after seven hundred years I'd get better at making friends."

Trick kissed him. "They don't understand, baby-boy. And they're jealous of what we have."

"I can't blame them, I guess." Bast reached up and nuzzled his throat. "There's nothing like you, Sweets. Nothing."

Trick chuckled. "I think they're jealous of me -- of what you give me."

"Give you? You feed me. You love me. You make me laugh. You make love to me like no one else." Bast kissed his throat, tears sliding down the back of his throat. "You came back for me."

"Oh, baby-boy..." Trick made a soft noise and buried his head in Bast's neck, holding on tight.

Bast snuggled close. "Let's go on a vacation. To the beach. Margaritas and nightclubs and sand. Give the guys a chance to cool off."

Trick laughed. "*You* want to go to the *beach*?"

"Well, yeah! I love to swim in the ocean!"

His Sweets continued to chuckle. "Oh, come on -- you've got to admit it's funny. Beaches and sun kind of go together, you know?"

Bast cackled. "Okay, okay. The mountains?"

If anything that made Trick laugh even harder. "You -- roughing it!" More laughter, Trick's breath huffed against his neck, warm and tickling. "Come on, tell me your perfect vacation wouldn't be spending the entire thing in a five star hotel suite with your every pleasure catered to you?"

"Oh, I could so handle that! Vegas? Dallas? Boston? You pick a place and I'll rent a car." Bast grinned. "Can you drive?"

Trick raised his head, grinning down at him. "You're serious, aren't you?"

Bast nodded. "Yeah. You got other plans?"

Trick's face grew serious. "I think I can clear my calendar."

"Then let's go." Bast nodded. "You pick a city and we'll go play."

"Anywhere? Las Vegas has always sounded like fun. We could gamble away all your money all night and make love all day."

Bast nodded and reached for his laptop. They needed this, needed a vacation, needed laughter and swimming pools and room service. "We can leave tomorrow. Want to fly or drive?"

Trick bounced on the bed next to him. "I've never flown."

"I don't do it often, but it's cool. How long shall we go? Two weeks?" Trick's enthusiasm was contagious, wonderful -- it made him feel excited and alive.

"That sounds great! Can I play the slots? And pretend to be James Bond at the baccarat tables?"

"Anything you want, Sweets." Bast made a few more arrangements and leaned over to give Trick a long kiss. "We leave tomorrow night. Cab picks us up at nine p.m. Wanna go shopping for luggage?"

"I'd rather go shopping for stuff to put into the luggage. Sparkles for you and black for me -- you can be my bond girl." Trick kissed him and laughed. "You have the best ideas."

"Yes. You're inspiring." Bast stood, heading for the

bathroom to shower. "Come on, lover. Let's get cleaned up and we'll go shopping."

# Chapter Twenty Three

Trick noticed the scars when he got out of the shower on their fourth day in Vegas. He'd become so used to them, he never saw them, but there were mirrors everywhere and the lights were so bright. The fine white lines that could just be tricks of the eye but on closer inspection proved to be fine scars.

There was one on his neck that was the most noticeable, the thickest and whitest. Then there was one on each wrist, one on the inside of his right thigh and one on his cock, near the base.

That one made him shiver, his cock filling rapidly and he had to go find Bast in the huge suite they were staying in. He had to find Bast right this very second because if his baby-boy didn't feed, he was just going to die.

"Bast?" he called out his lover's name as he left the bathroom.

"Yes, Sweets?" Bast's head popped up from beside the bed, disheveled and sexy as fuck.

He moaned, at least that's what he thought that noise was. The possibility did exist that it had been a whimper, but he liked to pretend that only happened during feeding.

"Hungry, baby-boy?"

Bast's eyes flashed, face tightening. "Always, Chosen."

"Good. Don't move."

He strode over to Bast, letting his cock lead him, eyes fastened on the red lips and white, white teeth of Bast's mouth.

Bast was vibrating, a low growl filling the room. "Chosen."

Another shudder went through him. Fuck, if Bast kept growling like that, kept calling him Chosen like that, he was going to come before he was even in Bast's mouth.

Those bright eyes shone at him, waited for him, hungry for him. Needing him.

At last he was in front of Bast, rubbing the tip of his cock against those thin, red lips. "Feed, baby-boy. Take me."

"Yes." Bast opened for him, tongue sliding over his shaft, lips tugging at the tip.

This time the noise was definitely a whimper and he could no more have kept still than he could have stopped breathing. He pushed deep, hands sliding into Bast's silky hair. Bast took him in, soft lips and tongue pulling, teeth scraping and teasing.

"Oh God, Bast. I love you."

Bast purred for him, hands reaching up to caress and hold. Those bright eyes stared up at him, fascinating and fascinated at once. He watched Bast as he started to move, hips pulling and pushing. He wet his lips, anticipation licking up and down along his spine.

Waiting for Bast to strike.

He could see those hot eyes, gleaming brighter and brighter with need. He moved faster, harder, and, as Bast's eyes turned completely yellow, Bast's hands gripped his ass, pulling him deep. The strike was quick, his lover biting hard.

Red filled his vision, pleasure overwhelming him. His head went back as he screamed, it was too big to contain, to try to hold in and he didn't even try. That mouth was pulling hard, drinking him down -- seed and blood intermingled.

Drinking him into Bast himself.

It moved so fast; it seemed no time at all before Bast was licking him, closing the wound, the connection. He collapsed down into his lover's arms with a small sob, pushing as close as he could.

"Mm... so good, Sweets." Bast's arms and legs surrounded him, holding him tight.

He nuzzled into Bast. "I hate it when it stops," he whispered. "When I'm not inside you anymore."

Bast nuzzled him right back. "You live inside me, Sweets. You always will."

"Is that what it means? Chosen?" He'd never asked before, never realized it might be something *more* than an endearment like 'Sweets' until their... friends had turned on them for it.

"Yes. It means that I need you, that no one will satisfy me like you can." Bast's hand stroked along his back, loving him. The bed was softer than theirs; the sound of the club on the eighteenth floor just starting up.

He grinned, arching into the touches like a cat. "Then you must be my Chosen."

"Am I? Yours?" Bast chuckled, lips nuzzling his neck. "You wear my marks, Sweets."

"And if I mark you? How long with the marks stay? A minute, an hour, a day?"

Bast nodded. "Unless we're going to get tattoos, Sweets, and I don't know if those will last more than thirty or forty years."

He nodded, fingers sliding over Bast's skin, pressing, making the skin briefly flare with color.

"Then how will they know?" he asked softly. "How will they know you're mine if I can't mark you?"

"Perhaps you will simply have to mark me again and again."

"Oh..." A shudder went through him. And then another. "Yes." He leaned forward, so slowly, pressing his lips to Bast's throat and sucking long and hard and slow.

"Oh..." Bast arched beneath him, moaning softly. "Sweets..."

He let his teeth scrape over Bast's skin, loving the way Bast jumped and jerked against him. "You like that? Like my teeth? Like knowing you're wearing my mark, even if it won't last?"

"Yes." Bast's voice was raspy, needing, cock hard and dark. "Yes, Sweets. Yes."

"If I could mark you permanently, that's what I'd do, you know? My teeth marks on your neck."

"Oh, fuck." Bast's hand moved to start pumping that sweet, stiff cock.

"No." He knocked Bast's hand away. "Inside me. While I bite you everywhere I can reach, putting my teeth marks on you."

Bast whimpered, arching. His eyes were wide open, lips parted as he gasped, completely lost in passion. "Sweets. Chosen. *Please*. Now, Trick. Now."

He shifted, dumping Bast back onto his ass and then climbed into his lover's lap. Moaning, he took Bast into himself. The stretch burned, the pain like sparks behind his eyes that soon became a deep red pleasure. Bast's groan was loud, filled the room. Those thin hips pushed up into him, so strong, so needy. He covered one thin shoulder with his mouth and bit down, hard but not sharp, leaving the imprint of his teeth without breaking skin.

"Trick!" Bast sobbed and twisted, hips rocking faster and harder.

"Yeah, yeah," he murmured, pleasure shooting up along his spine, lodging in his balls. He moved his head down, leaving a trail of heavy bite marks down to Bast's nipple.

Bast was wild, low growls sounding, his lover's eyes beginning to glow, face feral. He closed his mouth over that nipple, biting hard, wondering at what point the vampire would break and take what Trick was driving him to. A shiver of excitement shot through him.

"Chosen." The word was snarled, Bast's hands finding his hips. "Take care."

"Harder? Okay, I can do that." He moved to Bast's other nipple, the one over his heart, and bit as hard as he could.

His baby-boy screamed and lifted him. He grabbed Bast's shoulders as his back hit the bed, Bast's cock slamming deep as those sharp teeth buried themselves in his throat.

The world disappeared. The bed disappeared. What

he was doing disappeared. There was only the sound of his scream fighting the roar of his blood and the slide of Bast's cock inside him, over his gland, making him fly.

Bast filled him.

He filled Bast.

The circle spun and spun and spun.

It was perfect. The world slowly went black.

When he floated back, Bast was wrapped around him, purring and petting and so warm.

"My Chosen. Need you always. Need you. So good. My Sweets."

"Mmm..." He found one of his marks on Bast's skin, stroking it with his fingers. "Mine," he murmured with a soft smile.

"Yes, Sweets. Yours." He was given a soft, slow kiss.

"I love you, Bast."

"Yes. Trick. Forever." He got another kiss and another.

"Then I guess I don't need my marks to last."

"You just need to keep loving me." Bast's lips brushed over his eyelids. "You are my soul, Chosen, my life."

He slowly traced Bast's features, leaving the sharp teeth for last. "I am."

"Yes. My Chosen. My life." Bast gave him another kiss, tongue sliding deep, loving him. "You should rest. Sleep."

"You'll stay?" It wasn't really a questions, he knew Bast would.

"Forever."

"Like your marks on me." He smiled, eyes closing, fingers sliding over his own neck to feel the scars. They were there and they would never fade away.

Eternal. Like his Bast. Like them.
Forever.

# Chapter Twenty Four

Trick looked in the mirror, frowning. He had the beginnings of crow's feet. And laugh lines around his mouth. He wasn't young anymore and he didn't know when that had happened.

It wasn't like he was *old*, he just... didn't look like a kid anymore and it startled him. Bast still looked the same and he guessed for some reason, he thought he would as well, but every now and then he'd catch sight of himself in a mirror and realize he was older.

He wondered if it mattered to Bast. Did his lover mind the lines, the signs of aging? What would happen if he couldn't get it up anymore?

There was no doubt they'd have to leave eventually – go somewhere new where no one knew them, find somewhere people wouldn't care that he appeared to be a lot older than Bast. Maybe they'd go soon. Things had never been the same since Rose and Bael had pulled that stunt and he could feel the tug to leave, to start over somewhere new with Bast.

His baby-boy wandered out of the bathroom, steam puffing around the slender body, hair long enough to reach the thin hips. "Admiring again, Sweets? You are a fine looking man."

"Yeah? Do you still like how I look, Bast?"

He got a shocked look, those black-on-black eyes wide and bright. "What's not to like, Chosen?"

He shrugged and grinned, arms looping around the slender waist. "I just don't look the same as when we first hooked up, you know?"

Bast's arms twined around his neck, towel falling away as he was snuggled up against. "Yeah, you're taller."

He laughed, cock firming, pressing against the zipper of his jeans. "Got more stamina now, too," he pointed out.

"Mmm... You make me just as hungry now as you did that first night. Make me ache." One sharp finger traced his jaw, the scars on his throat.

He moaned pulling Bast close as he let his head drop back, exposing his neck to his lover. The snarl was low, sharp, familiar and as necessary as breathing. Bast vibrated in his arms, fangs resting on his throat. "My Chosen..."

Trick shuddered, so close to the edge, just waiting for Bast to push him off. Some things, it seemed, didn't change.

"I love you." A hot tongue slid over his skin, Bast's cock hard as steel against him. "Hungry..."

"Feed then, baby-boy. Please. Love it when you feed..." He whimpered, pulled their hips together rhythmically.

"Need your life inside me. So rich." Bast groaned,

sobbed, bit deep and fed.

He hollered as he came, pleasure slamming through him. Years passed by and it still hit him so hard. The bite and pull easing, Bast carried him to their bed, purring and rubbing against him. Bast was so hot, burning as the blood rocking through the thin body. He whimpered again, cock growing, Bast making him hungry even as he fed.

The wound was closed, then a sharp bite nipped at his collarbone, tongue lapping at his blood. His body jerked, cock solid again, his jeans uncomfortable now.

"Mmm... Sweets." His nipple was snagged next, the bites playful, bright against his skin.

Groaning, he shifted, hands moving to take off his jeans.

"Chosen. Need you. Want you always." Bast whispered it like it was a prayer, hot and wet against his skin.

"I want you, too, Bast. So much." He got his jeans off and slid his fingers over Bast's head, fingers tracing the high cheekbones, sliding across the soft lips.

Bast's eyes glowed for him, bright and green, and his fingertips were nibbled and licked, palms nuzzled.

"You always make me feel so good," he murmured, body rippling beneath Bast.

"You are my lover, my friend, my Chosen. How else would I have you feel?"

He chuckled. "You'd have me feel you."

Bast blinked, then low, happy laughter echoed through the room. "Yes. Fuck, yes. Always!"

Grinning he rolled them, pushing against Bast, moaning as his cock slid over warm skin. Bast stretched out beneath him, purring and moaning, arching up into his skin.

"And I have to say," he whispered against Bast's ear, "that you feel fantastic."

"Mm... Sweet-talker." Bast's voice was a whimper.

"I try." He bit Bast's lobe, worrying the soft flesh between his teeth.

"Trick..." The thin body jerked, arched, neck tilting.

"Oh, you want me to bite you here, too, do you?" He spoke the words against Bast's skin, slowly making his way down along the long, thin throat. He nipped and bit at the skin, fastening his lips around Bast's pulse point and sucking hard, rhythmically as if feeding.

"Trick. Fuck. Sweets." Bast started moving in time with the suction, rocking and moaning, hands tangling in his hair.

He loved pushing Bast, loved making his lover lose control and want desperately. He moved his hips, slamming down against that thin body, their cocks sliding roughly together.

"Yes. More. Oh, Trick. More." Bast was shuddering, hot in his hands.

He bit and humped, pushing as hard as he could. Fuck, he loved his baby-boy, so much. Bast came, crying out his name, the word echoing with hunger and love and incredible, unbearable need. He shuddered, climax ripped from his body by that sound of that need.

Bast wrapped around him, purring and close. Happy.

He relaxed against his lover. Maybe he'd have the mirror taken out. He liked the way he looked in Bast's eyes just fine.

# Chapter Twenty Five

The music blared, beat vibrating the neon pillars, vibrating the walls, vibrating his body.

Dressed in vinyl, hair dyed dark purple, lipstick to match, Bast was waiting to be found.

Ten years since his Sweets had found him, fucked him and now he waited. He'd left fifty bucks and a note saying only 'Hide and Seek, Sweets' on the bed. Then he'd hurried out to see how long it took his lover to find him.

The nightclub had changed owners a half-dozen times, the decor was different, the music had changed -- but the columns were still there, the nightclub crowd always looked the same and the whiskey was still good.

And there he was, black jeans tight, t-shirt tighter, walking balls first, hips rolling. Trick went right up to the bar and leaned with his back against it, watching the crowd lazily. When the bartender put down his shot,

Trick handed the man Bast's fifty.

Oh, fuck, Trick was still the sexiest thing he'd ever seen. Maybe even sexier now that the desperation and bitterness had turned to confidence and loose-limbed satisfaction.

His cock rose just watching his Sweets' stomach ripple as he threw back the whiskey. Oh yeah, definitely sexier now.

Trick left the bar and slowly slunk across to the dance floor, standing at the edge of it, hips swaying with the beat. Trick's eyes wandered over the crowd as if searching and a small smile played about his lips.

Bast chuckled, perched comfortably, letting the beat of the music and the anticipation and the sex and hunger that was his Trick set his nerves afire.

Trick frowned and then pouted, sighing dramatically, turning to go.

Turning back again, Trick started moving across the dance floor in what seemed on the surface to be a random pattern, but it was a pattern that slowly, inexorably, led him toward the column Bast was perched upon.

It took forever -- or maybe just two songs -- and then Trick was standing by his column, still not looking up.

Turning, Trick leaned against the column and began to move against it, body flowing to the slow, hypnotic beat. Reaching back, Trick grabbed the column and slowly slid his hands along it until they were up over his head and then slid back down again.

Bast moaned, slowly slinking down the column, unwilling and unable to resist his lover's allure. When he reached Trick, he plastered their bodies together, lips reaching up, begging a kiss.

Trick chuckled, the sound pure sex. "You interrupted

my floor show." He wasn't given time to answer, Trick's lips covered his, mouth open wide, hungry.

He groaned into the kiss, hips grinding against Trick, his cock hard enough to cut glass. Trick tasted like blood and meat and whiskey and sheer fucking desire. Trick turned him until his back was pressed against the column, the heavy body pressed up against him. The music changed again, something fast and wild and Trick drew back, grinning wickedly.

"I know you remember what comes next."

"Oh, yeah." He smiled up, as hungry now as he was then. "So, you found me. What do you want for your prize, Sweets?"

Trick grabbed the column above his head and pressed close, erection hot and hard against him. "On your knees, Bast. I want you to suck me."

Oh, yes. Bast slid to his knees, eager and ready for the feel of Trick on his tongue. His fingers found the zipper of Trick's black jeans and pulled, letting the thick erection spring free.

Trick was staring down at him, eyes dark with passion, the purple column reflected in them. Lean hips pushed Trick's heavy cock against his lips. He swallowed it down with a happy noise, sucking hard and firm, letting his fangs graze along the sensitive skin.

Bast could hear Trick's moan over the music as one of his Sweets' hands slid into his hair, holding him in place as Trick started to thrust into his mouth. The music was loud, the crowd thick, chattering and laughing and none of it mattered as Trick groaned and came down his throat.

He swallowed Trick down and then stood, tucking his lover away as their lips met in a long, whiskey and come-flavored kiss.

When the kiss ended Trick licked his own lips, eyes hot and sultry. "So did you like that, Bast? You want some more of it?"

"I'll take all you've got to offer, Sweets." He leaned forward, licking Trick's lips with a grin. "You still taste good."

Trick chuckled again and his arms looped around Bast's waist, pulling their hips close as he danced them into the crowd, swaying slowly. "You going to taste me properly, baby-boy?"

Bast purred and burrowed his face into the low curve of Trick's neck, nipping just enough for his Chosen to feel. "You mean me sucking you down while I'm on my knees in a nightclub wasn't proper?"

Trick's breath hitched and his Sweets jerked against his hips and then Trick chuckled again, the deep sound shivering down his spine. "Not a single thing was proper about that, Bast. That's what made it so much fun."

He chuckled, leaning back to look up into the beloved face and press their hips tighter together. When he'd tasted his Sweets the first time they'd looked close to the same age -- Bast smaller and younger, but not surprisingly so. Now, Trick was in his prime, tall and muscular and Bast was still, well, Bast-sized. In ten more years, maybe five, they wouldn't be able to do this in public without someone being suspicious.

"Is it still as good now? As it was that first time, I mean."

"Fuck no." Trick grinned down at him. "It's so much better than it was back then. Fuck, I was such a prick."

"You were still sexy as fuck, Sweets, and tasted like whiskey and chocolate." He winked, letting his hunger show for a second. "I will admit that you taste sweeter now, more addictive."

"You're pretty damn addictive yourself," murmured Trick. His Sweets took his mouth, the kiss deep and long, not caring where they were or who saw them.

By the time Trick's lips left him, he was aching, rubbing against Trick with hunger. "That... oh fuck, Sweets, your kisses have got to be listed as an illegal drug."

"A lot harder to come by though, if your name isn't Bast." Trick was moving them slowly among the crowd on the dance floor, hips moving sensuously.

"Lucky for me." His fingers were tangled in the hair at Trick's nape, his cock rubbing against the strong thighs. "Want you, Sweets. Want to feel you inside me."

"Well, I'd offer to do you up against that column, but I have a feeling that might get us arrested."

"So practical." He chuckled, leaning up to take another not-quite gentle bite of Trick's throat. "So even-headed."

Trick groaned. "So about to do it anyway."

"Mmm... I don't look good in orange jumpsuits and somehow I don't think they'd understand my particular needs."

"Then let's get out of here before it becomes an issue, baby-boy." Trick's hand found his, his Sweets practically dragging him off the dance floor.

He followed his lover happily out into the cold, holding onto his Sweets for all he was worth.

"Think you can wait 'til we get home?" Trick asked, arm going around his shoulders, pulling him close. "Or should we risk frostbite in a back alley?"

"Mmm... let's go home. That way I can feed with you hot and hard inside me." He snuggled close, one hand reaching up to stroke Trick's throat.

Trick shuddered and walked faster. "I like the way your mind works."

They hurried home, laughing and teasing and touching, so much happier and more free than that first night, but still with the same breathless anticipation, the hunger and need only grown over time.

They were both shivering a little when they made it to the elevator, Bast lifting his face for a kiss as soon as the key was turned and the downward journey started. Trick shoved him up against the back wall, mouth taking his, body hard against him. Bast wrapped around Trick, arms around his throat, legs around his waist, tongue around his tongue.

Fuck, but his Sweets tasted like heaven.

Trick started to thrust with his hips, pushing him into the side of the elevator, making it clang noisily. He groaned into Trick's mouth, each of Trick's thrusts making his balls ache, bringing him closer and closer to climax. He captured Trick's tongue with his lips, sucking it hard, pulling his Sweets' flavor inside him.

The elevator stopped moving, coming to a stop with a heavy groan, but Trick didn't release him, didn't stop humping him against the wall. His hands gripped Trick's shoulders, squeezing hard as he screamed out his orgasm, eyes rolling up as the sensation slammed through him. Trick kept moving against him, keeping him shivering in pleasure's hold.

"Oh, fuck. Good, Sweets. *So* good." His mouth found Trick's throat, pulling and sucking, teeth just teasing.

Trick groaned and wrapped his arms around Bast's butt, standing and walking him out of the elevator toward the bed. "I can't wait to fuck you, baby-boy."

"Mm... yes. Yes, please, Sweets. Need you." He licked his way up to Trick's ear, nipping at the lobe.

Trick dropped them both onto the bed, his Sweets' weight heavy against him. Trick pressed into his neck, mouth hot and wet, breath a warm breeze. Blunt fingers pushed into his tight pants, tugging the vinyl off his legs. He tugged at Trick's t-shirt, exposing the firm muscles for his touch. Wriggling out of his pants, Bast kicked them aside, suddenly desperate for the feel of skin on skin.

Trick backed away long enough to pull off his shirt and jeans, barely giving Bast the time he needed to take off his shirt before slamming him back into the bed, body hot and hard against him.

"Fuck, yes..." The words were gasped into Trick's mouth, his legs reaching up to wrap around his Sweets' hips. The blaze of skin against skin was perfect -- hot and right and erotic as hell.

Trick's arms locked onto the bed on either side of his head, his Sweets' cock hard and insistent against him, pushing as that hot tongue fucked him. He reached down, tilting his hips and pressing the head of Trick's cock against his opening, letting the drops of fluid leaking from his Sweets spread over him. Then he ground up, grunting into their kiss as the head of the hard flesh popped inside.

Trick growled and started to fuck him, long, hard strokes that he could feel all the way up his spine and down to his toes. So good. His Sweets made him fly, made him believe and love and oh... He looked up into the face grown taut with pleasure. "Make me so hungry, Sweets."

Trick's eyes opened, glazed and unfocussed. "Oh yeah, baby-boy. Feed."

"Yes." The hiss sounded only a breath before he leaned up, fangs striking true and deep, blood filling his mouth.

Trick thrust deep, body shaking as he screamed like he was being murdered. Or like he was experiencing the best orgasm he'd ever had since the last time Bast had fed. He fed happily, body taking each of the sweet, shuddering jerks of Trick's body as he pulled sustenance and pleasure from his Sweets in equal amounts.

Trick's weight grew heavier, arms finally buckling as he collapsed heavily against Bast. "Love you, Bast," Trick whispered, voice soft.

"Oh, I love you, too, Sweets." He smiled, wrapping his arms around his lover and holding tight. So much nicer than the first time, so much sweeter and right.

Trick was still buried inside him, licking lazily at his ear.

"Mmm... could spend the rest of eternity just like this, Trick."

"I don't know... it's nice to have you on top now and then," Trick teased, tongue sliding into his ear, breath hot and loud.

"Mm..." He nodded, grinning. "...and the sucking's pretty good, too. Guess we're gonna need a lot of fucking eternities."

"Sounds perfect to me."

Yes. Yes, it did. And Bast would be damned before he wasted another second of this sweet reality wishing for it.

Rolling Trick over onto his back, he began to work on filling this reality with more loving.

# Epilogue

Trick watched as the sun set over the water. Just another minute and then Bast could join him and they could have their first night on the beach. He grinned. Only Bast would want to live somewhere that people traditionally went to for the sun.

He waited, waited for Bast to come to him.

"Sweets? Is it time yet?" Bast's voice was rough, sleepy and lonely. The echoes sounded different here, above ground.

"Come look at your sea, baby-boy." He reached back for his lover.

A slender hand slid into his, Bast wearing a thin robe -- one of his, it was swallowing his lover up, but Bast liked them, liked his smell on them -- and pressing tight against his side. "Oh... Oh, it's beautiful. You're happy?"

He wrapped his arm around Bast, bending to kiss the

sweet lips. "I'm with you. I couldn't be happier."

"Mmm... flirt." Bast purred, gasping as the wind blew the long, fine black hair. "It's so different here. So *alive.*"

"Yeah? So you're happy? This is what you wanted?" He looked down into the dark eyes, needing to know, wanting Bast to be happy.

"Trick." Bast looked up at him, eyes old and quiet, the sorrow hidden in them perpetual. "I'm as happy as I can be, Chosen."

He closed his eyes; he couldn't bear to see Bast so sad. "I love you," he whispered, lips sliding over Bast's.

Bast opened to him, tongue sliding over his lips. "Chosen..."

"I love you," he whispered again, closing their mouths together, taking a long kiss.

Bast melted into him, soft sounds pushing into his lips, little sounds that meant love and need and please all rolled up together.

He pushed Bast's -- his -- robe open, hands sliding over the pale skin. "You hungry, baby-boy? It was a long trip -- do you need?"

"Oh..." Bast shivered for him, gasped. "Yes. So much. Time change, you know. *So* hungry." Dark eyes turned golden, shining at him. "Chosen..."

He raised his chin, eyes still on Bast as he pulled his lover's mouth to his throat. "Feed, baby-boy. Take what's yours."

"Mine. I love you, Sweets. Always." Bast was vibrating in his hands, fangs trailing along his skin, teasing them both.

He spread his legs slightly, setting his feet in the sand, bracing himself to hold them up when his world went red. A sweet shudder went through him, anticipation making him hard.

"I can smell you and underneath that, the sea. Fucking *sexy*, Trick." Then Bast bit deep, sending him flying.

He screamed into the wind, the pleasure coursing through him as strongly as ever. Every time was like the first time, strong and good and overwhelming.

Suddenly the pleasure faded, Bast licking his throat closed. When he moaned, Bast shook his head, hair flying. "Going to take you slow. Again and again. All night."

He moaned, body trembling at the thought. "We'd better go lie down then, Bast. I don't think my legs'll hold out. I'm getting old."

"No?" Bast made a soft noise, then those teeth scraped his throat again. "Fuck it, I can't wait."

Then the rush hit him again, stronger this time, more fierce. He screamed again, legs buckling. Pleasure was red and hot and two hearts beating with the same blood. Bast kept him sinking, beating, floating, every cell in his body orgasming again and again. His screams faded to soft sobs, body shaking with the intensity of it until finally red faded into black.

When he woke, he was in their new bed, warm and safe, Bast curled up behind him, holding him.

"Love you, baby-boy," he murmured.

"Love you." Bast's hands stroked over his belly. "Rest now; you were awake all day. Sleep."

"Gotta get back on schedule. All this travel's messed my internal clock up again."

"Yeah. You'll adjust. 'sides the ocean is beautiful in the sunshine and you'll need to go exploring." Bast nuzzled him gently, voice low and dreamy, fingers tangled into his hair, the gold and silver strands all mixed together now. "We should find me another name, another person to be."

"You'll always be my baby-boy."

"Always, Chosen, until the end of time."

He covered Bast's hand with his own, fingers twining together.

The end of time.

He could live with that.

943792

Printed in Great Britain by
Amazon.co.uk, Ltd.,
Marston Gate.